White Rabbit's Tail

& other yuletide ghost stories

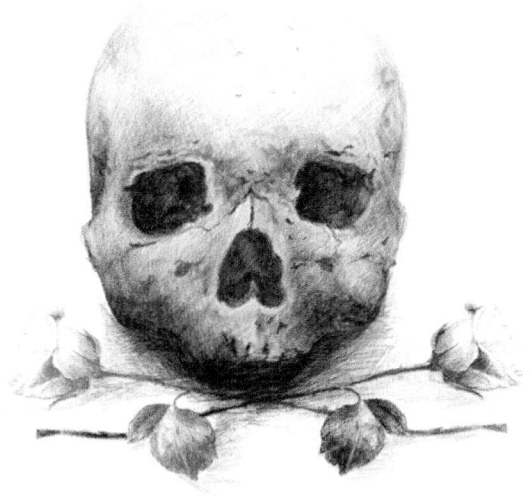

Heavenly Flower Publishing Authors

First published in 2025 by Heavenly Flower Publishing

White Witch's Hat & other yuletide ghost stories
Copyright © 2025 Heavenly Flower Publishing authors

Cover and chapter thumbnail designs © 2025 Leilanie Stewart: Designed using elements from Canva Pro
Internal artwork © 2025 Beata Milewska

ISBN: 9798270111403

The characters, events, names and places used in this book are fictitious or used fictitiously. Any resemblance to real persons, living or dead is coincidental.

No part of this book may be reproduced in any form or by any means without the express written permission of the publisher.

All rights reserved

Thank you for supporting independent publishing.

Bindweed Anthologies/ Heavenly Flower Publishing
Website: https://bindweedmagazine.wordpress.com
Edited by: Leilanie Stewart and Joseph Robert

WHITE WITCH'S HAT
& other Yuletide ghost stories

Heavenly Flower Publishing Authors

Editor's note

As this is an anthology, there may be some content that is troubling for some readers. Content disclaimer for reader discretion: adult themes.

Bindweed proudly features writers from all over the English-speaking world, therefore there may be differences in spelling and punctuation, and even in meaning.

4.12.25

To Laura

Yuletide greetings and solstice blessings!

Enjoy the scare...
Leilanie Stewart

Contents

	The meaning of White Witch's Hat	i
1	**Leilanie Stewart** White Witch's Hat	Pg 1
2	**Joseph Robert** Bauble	Pg 12
3	**Sarah Das Gupta** Skating on Thin Ice	Pg 15
4	**Kevin MacAlan** The Plumicorn Affair	Pg 21
5	**Steve Cashell** Southbound Traveller	Pg 31
6	**Matthew J. Richardson** The Kinmount Straight	Pg 42
7	**Michael P. Boettcher** What the Fire Keeps	Pg 48
8	**Eolas Pellor** Home for Christmas	Pg 57

9	**Ria Cabral**	Pg 67
	The Caroler at the Gate	
10	**Tim Newton Anderson**	Pg 73
	Snow Angel	
11	**Alice Baburek**	Pg 82
	Echoes of a Lost Soul	
12	**Hadyn Adams**	Pg 85
	The Proof of the Pudding is in the Eating	
13	**Evan Baughfman**	Pg 94
	The Yeti's Claw	
14	**Plamen Vasilev**	Pg 106
	The Holly King's Curse	
15	**Monti Sturzaker**	Pg 113
	The Wine Coloured Dress	
16	**Subham Rai**	Pg 117
	The Holly Locket Curse	
17	**Sarah Hozumi**	Pg 126
	The Second Tree	
18	**Amber Willis**	Pg 136
	Grab the Christmas Cookies	
19	**Christmas Mourning**	Pg 140
	Callum J. McCready	
20	**Nathan McKee**	Pg 150
	The Gift	
21	**Amy Finlay**	Pg 156
	The diary of Elisha Kent Kane – Arctic Explorer	
	Author Bios	**Pg 163**
	About Bindweed Anthologies	**Pg 167**

The meaning of White Witch's Hat

This anthology marks a change back to the original format of Bindweed Magazine, as it started life creeping across the great fence of life back in April 2016. Inspired by the many nicknames for convolvulus arvensis or common bindweed, previous issues have had titles such as:

>Issue 1 – Morning Glory
>Issue 2 – Bellbine
>Issue 3 – Creeping Jenny
>Issue 4 – Waywind
>Issue 5 – Wild Lily
>Issue 6 – Robin-run-the-hedge
>Issue 7 – Lady-jump-out-of-bed
>Issue 8 – Laplove

And previous anthologies, such as:

>Bindweed Anthology (2018) Devil's Guts
>Bindweed Anthology (2025) Withywind

White Witch's Hat is another colloquial nickname for common bindweed and provided inspiration through the sinister connotations that such a moniker conjured. A spooky seasonal story began to spread like weeds in the mind.

Here at Bindweed, we're idealistic folks, and we strive to support fellow authors with their writing careers too. Once the titular *White Witch's Hat* story was fully formed, we decided, why not invite other authors to contribute similarly spooky yuletide stories in a themed collection?

Well, why not?

Enjoy!

1

Leilanie Stewart

White Witch's Hat

Gordon drew the curtains and light streamed into his living room. Snow flurries swirled in the air. Would it be a white Christmas this year? Possibly, though it was only the twenty first of December. Maybe if it got heavy, and settled on the ground, it would last for the next four days.

His gaze panned across his garden, admiring the holly bushes that threw splashes of red amidst the green spiky leaves. A fresh sprig would look great on the front door wreath. Lilian would have wanted that. She took so much pride in her garden – their garden – before she… before she…

What a year it had been. The loneliest year since her passing on Christmas Eve the previous year. Yes. His mind was made up. A splash of colour would add some festive cheer. Lilian would have wanted him to get his mind off things and to continue with their traditions.

Gordon hurried into the hall and pulled on his coat and boots. A flurry of fat snowflakes hit his face as he stepped into the garden. But his smile at the bright red berries faltered as his focus swept to the left, to the dividing fence between his garden and the neighbour's. Twisting green vines snaked all over the fence, the white flowering weeds inclining their trumpet-like heads towards him, as though mocking him. Bindweed flowers never grew when Lilian tended the garden, but Gordon knew he had let a lot of things slide during his year of mourning; including her beloved plants.

Wait a minute; why were Bindweed flowers growing in winter? Didn't they grow in spring and summer? He wasn't a gardener by any means, but he knew enough to recognise that Yule wasn't growing season.

Gordon shrugged to himself as he stomped across to the fence. No matter the reason for their presence, they were unwanted.

"Nasty nuisance!" He grabbed a handful of the weeds and dragged them off the fence, tearing the vines until none were left. "Into the bin with you!"

He plucked a few sprigs of holly, his mind now set on getting a nice cup of tea and slice of Yule log before fixing the door wreath.

As Gordon turned to go inside his warm, welcoming house, a flash of white at the corner of his eye made him turn. He could have sworn a tall woman, wearing a long, white dress and wide-brimmed white hat, had been standing behind him at the bottom of the garden by the gate; but it must have been his imagination. Just a trick of the light in the snowstorm.

***

Three days. Three days, came the whisper on the wind.

Gordon sat bolt upright, his heart hammering. Had that whisper been in a dream, or words spoken by someone? Who: his neighbour? If so, they would have had to shout very loudly to be heard through the wall between their two semi-detached houses.

Three days. What did that mean? Christmas Eve?

He shook his head to clear his head of slumber, swung his legs out of bed and put his slippers on. TV would be the necessary remedy to get his mind off whatever message the 'three days' meant.

As soon as he went downstairs, Gordon put the kettle on straightaway, out of habit more than anything else.

"Lily, would you like me to fix you some toast?" he called.

Oh wait; that was out of habit too. He hung his head, his question floating on dead air.

"*Yes,*" came a faint response.

Gordon gasped and dropped the mug he had lifted off the counter, the ceramic shattering on the tiled kitchen floor. Instinct made him spin, one hand clasped against his hammering heart.

"Lily?" He shuffled in his slippers along the hallway and into the living room, in the direction of the faint voice. "Lily, is that you?"

As he stepped into the living room doorway, the breath caught in Gordon's throat. Over by the fireplace, her back to him, stood a glimmering outline of his deceased wife, Lilian. Her hair tumbled loose over her shoulders, and she wore the nightdress she had been wearing on that fateful night.

"Lily," he croaked. "How can this be?"

She shook her head, her face mournful. "I don't know. I really can't say."

"Are you – that is to say – well, you must be," he started.

"A ghost," she finished. "I suppose."

"But why? Were you here the whole time?"

A pensive expression appeared on her opaque features. "No. It was as though I was asleep, and I've just woken up from a very long dream."

Gordon ventured a step into the room. "A dream of what?"

"Recurring dreams, about lots of things." She looked towards the garden. "A white Christmas tree, about six feet tall, turning into a giant hat, like the kind that witches wear in children's fairy tales."

"A White Witch's hat?" Gordon repeated, trying to understand.

Lilian nodded. "A whisper would call to me from inside the White Witch's hat, and it was so enticing, so intriguing that I couldn't resist walking towards it. And when I went to it – then, blackness. Nothing. Until the next time."

"And what happened the next time?" he urged.

She narrowed her misty eyes, and Gordon sensed her trying to recall. "More dreams of the White Witch's hat consuming me. Sometimes there would be a feeling of being squeezed tight, and at other times, only the irresistible pull of the hat."

Gordon paused, making sense of what she had to say. "When you say 'squeezed', do you mean, like, how you died of asphyxiation?"

She tilted her head to one side. "I'm not sure, darling. I don't rightly remember the details of my death."

"The official cause of death said asphyxiation, but it's a mystery, my dear. Our carbon monoxide alarm didn't sound, and besides, I would have died too if noxious gas was the cause." He inhaled, thinking. "There were no marks on your throat to suggest strangulation. I simply came home from the grocery store and found you in the wicker chair in the conservatory."

She smiled. "I love that chair. Tell me you didn't get rid of it?"

"I couldn't bear to look at it after what happened. I moved it out into the shed," he sighed.

Lilian was crestfallen. "Well, it was probably for the best." Her face brightened as she walked towards the living room window and peered between a gap in the curtains. "Oh Gordon, how lovely! I see you've kept my garden nice and neat."

He couldn't help grinning. "Yes, dear, I knew you would have wanted that. I took a few sprigs of holly for the wreath too. But the strangest thing happened. You'll never guess what was growing on the fence between our garden and the neighbours'."

Gordon gave a dramatic pause, anticipating her reaction to the dratted weeds.

"What, darling?" she said quietly.

"Bindweed. All over the place." His eyes crinkled as his grin stretched wider, expecting her face to crumple in outrage. She hated weeds in her immaculate garden. Hated them with a passion.

Instead, her face fell clear of any expression. Her mouth became a taut line. Her eyes were round and blank. Her arms fell limp at her sides, and she began to walk towards the hallway.

"Lily? Lily, where are you going?"

Did she not believe him, and was going to the garden to look for herself? Gordon followed her into the hall, but she was gone.

"Lily, oh no! Lily my love! What have I done?"

It was his fault. Teasing her had backfired. It had caused her to become so upset, she had disappeared. Had she used up her ethereal energy visiting him, and now she had burned out, like a Christmas candle snuffing out in a cold winter breeze?

***

Gordon padded across the snow-covered back garden towards the shed. He hadn't given much thought to Lily's old wicker chair for the past year, as the memory of finding her in it was too painful, but now he had an overwhelming need to see it. Not just to look at it, but to touch it; run his hands over it, get a sense for the wood, and to sit in it, allowing his body to fill its space.

His fingers fumbled with the cold metal padlock, but he managed to twist the key and snap it open. As he pulled back the door and looked inside the shed, a loud gasp escaped his chest and he clasped a hand to his heart.

A tall, young woman sat in the wicker chair. She wore a long white satin gown that looked like a nightdress, made of a fabric too flimsy for winter. It reached to her ankles and was cut in a low V across her ample cleavage. A white pointed hat with a wide, floppy brim cast her eyes in shadow. At first glance, it seemed like a witch's hat, but on closer inspection had the trumpet-like shape of a flower head; much like the pesky Bindweed flowers invading his garden, if he were honest. The woman had long, silver-blue hair the colour of glaciers, and when she raised her chin to look at him, Gordon saw her steely-grey eyes that fixed him in an unblinking stare.

"How did you get in here?" He demanded. "What do you want?"

"Two," she said, in barely more than a whisper. "Days."

That voice; that whisper. It was the same one he had heard in his bedroom the previous night. The same voice that had roused him from a peaceful sleep.

Gordon couldn't put his finger on what it was that unnerved him about the strange young woman. "Get out of here," he cried. The words poured out of his mouth before the reasonable part of his mind could filter them.

He turned to hold the shed door open for the woman to leave, and when he looked back, she was gone.

A whimper escaped his throat. "Dear Lord, protect me. A witch! A witch, or a ghost, or a fiend, and in my own shed too!"

***

Gordon was beside himself with fear. Who could he go to for help? He and Lily didn't have any children and his brother, Samuel, had passed many years ago.

Church. He would have to go and ask the vicar for advice. Yes, that was the best place to go for a spiritual crisis.

Gordon wasted no time. Already wearing his coat and boots, he hurried along the side path connecting front and back gardens, then without a backward glance, turned onto the street and made for the church. Snow swirled around his face, and he blinked fat flakes from his eyelashes.

As if heaven-sent, the vicar came out of the church. White flakes of snow settled on the vicar's grey woollen coat and green scarf coiled around his neck as he stopped to lock the door. Nothing unusual about that; it wasn't a service day, so he probably only had office matters to attend to before closing up early. Gordon was in luck; he could catch him for a brief chat and then they could both get home before the blizzard.

"Hello there, Peter," Gordon called through the growing gale, only twenty feet away from the vicar.

The vicar turned. He didn't smile. Unusual; Peter was always in high spirits. The change caused Gordon to pause, before shuffling onwards, closing the distance between them.

"Peter, I wonder if you could lend an ear for a moment. You see, I'm in need of some guidance on a spiritual matter of sorts—"

"I can't help you," Peter interrupted. "I can't even help myself."

A wet gurgling sound emitted from the vicar's throat as he feebly clutched at his neck, as though his throat had been suddenly constricted. His eyes began to bulge, and his skin turned puce, as he choked, fingers grappling to no avail.

"Oh Lord!" Gordon cried.

His instinct kicked in. He pulled at Peter's fingers, but they were locked on his throat as tight as a boa constrictor. The vicar gagged, his tongue protruding as veins sprouted on his temples. The capillaries in his eyes began to burst, the corneas swimming in blood.

The vicar dropped to the ground, and Gordon was left with his arms extended into swirling snow.

Before his eyes, the spindrift intensified into a snow devil. In the midst of the swirling white vortex, the White Witch appeared. Her satin dress clung to her slender figure as she strode through the thickening snow. She stood over the vicar's body and removed her hat, holding it above his head. Silent words poured from her mouth, but it was clear they were for the vicar's deceased body only.

A faint, shimmering light emerged from the crown of the dead vicar's head and formed into wavering smoke ribbons. They floated upwards, into the wide brim of the White Witch's hat. Gordon recognised Peter's likeness among the smoke ribbons; he could discern the shadowy features of the vicar's eyes, nose and mouth, twisted in despair as his soul disappeared into the hat.

"No! Peter!"

After the vicar's soul had been sucked into the hat, the White Witch placed it back on top of her long silvery-blue tresses. One corner of her mouth twitched into a smirk, and she fixed him with her unnatural steely-grey eyes.

"Two days," she hissed, smooth as a snake.

Gordon shrieked before turning and running for his life.

***

Knock, knock, knock.

Trembling, he fumbled with the latch, and allowed the front door to open as far as the safety chain would allow. Not that the safety chain was any good against a witch, but it had provided meagre emotional safety throughout the night and that was better than nothing.

Of course, a witch didn't need to knock–

In the cold morning brightness, Gordon saw the police sergeant standing on his doorstep.

"Oh, sergeant," he gasped. "Am I glad to see you."

The sergeant narrowed his eyes. "For what reason?"

"I'm not sure if I can explain it. I can barely understand it myself," Gordon babbled.

"I *hope* you can explain it," said the sergeant. "I'll need to bring you down to the station for a few questions, I'm afraid."

Gordon blinked, processing the sergeant's words. "This must be about Peter?"

"I see you're under no illusions. In that case, we'll need you to explain how the vicar came to be lying in front of the church, strangled to death."

Gordon made a strangled noise himself. "Surely you aren't implying that – well, there's no way that a man of my age could – what I mean to say is–"

"Just come to the station with us, Gordon, and let's keep things simple," said the sergeant, in the unfriendliest tone he had ever heard him speak during the fifty years he had lived in the village.

Frozen thoughts raced through Gordon's head as the sergeant drove him towards the station, in the back of the police car, like a common criminal. He had never been questioned by the police in his life. Now he was a prisoner of both the police, and worse, the witch.

Thank goodness he wasn't led into a cell. Instead of a room with bars, he was taken into a small office. The décor was spartan, with only one medium-sized Christmas tree to provide meagre Yuletide cheer.

"Wait here." The harsh tone of the sergeant's words was acrid in his ears, a reminder that he was a prime suspect for murder.

The door slammed shut, leaving him alone.

Heat began to creep across his face. At first, he thought it was the injustice of his confinement, but as a tightness formed around his neck, his fingers fumbled over his throat and to his horror, Gordon felt tight vines coiled around his neck. An image of the vicar's last moments the previous day popped into his head. Peter had been wearing his grey overcoat and had a green scarf wrapped around his neck. Gordon understood. Not a green scarf; green bindweed vines in tight loops around his throat.

"Gordy. Gordy, fight it." Muffled words reached him from beyond the flower petals.

"Lily?"

Her voice gave him strength. He had to fight for his life. Fight the bindweed vines that would lead to his doom – for body and for soul. He had to fight the witch. Destroy her asphyxiating vines before they destroyed him.

"Begone, wretched witch! Trouble me no more!"

Gordon flung his arms outwards, ripping the bindweed coils from his neck. The constriction on his neck disappeared, leaving him gasping for air. The ghost of his wife, Lily, stood smiling before him, and misty tears glistened in the corners of her spectral eyes.

"You did it Gordy," she gushed. "Now you won't suffer my fate. I remember now. She comes for those who kill her precious *convolvulus arvensis* – you, me, and the vicar. But you did it, Gordy, you outwitted her!"

But then, a whisper cut through the oppressive air.

"Your day," crooned the White Witch's voice from behind.

Gordon turned and peered over his left shoulder. The fairy lights that had circled the Christmas tree had morphed into thick, twisting vines laced with white trumpet-like flowers. *White Witch's Hat*, common bindweed flowers; known for their persistence, and aggression. They snaked around him, pinning his arms to his sides, wrapping their twin stems tight around his neck. Tighter.

"Oh no!" Lily cried. "The White Witch's hat! It comes for those who smite it…"

A smothering, claustrophobic sensation engulfed him, as though an invisible plastic bag had been placed over his head. By way of reflex, he looked up and felt his blood run cold. A giant, preternatural white flower hung over his head. Yellow sepals like corn-snakes reached for him and an overpowering earthy scent, the aroma of the grave, wafted around him, lulling him into a stupor.

The words drifted into his ears as Gordon felt his body slump forwards. The momentary heaviness of his own weight suddenly lifted, and like a hook pulling at the crown of his head, he felt himself rushing upwards into white light.

"I'm sorry, Lily, she got me," he tried to say, but wasn't sure if the words reached her.

"It's okay, my love. We're together again, at least."

But their exchange was cut short by the White Witch, her voice more resonant now beyond the veil.

"Winter solstice, life is cruel
Flowers wither under Yule,
Then light returns, days get longer
Holly fades, oak grows stronger.

Roots lie deep, meaning that
If you see The White Witch's Hat
And kill her beauty, you will find
She repays the smite in kind.

For half a year, she comes to reap
The lives of those who seek to keep
Morning Glory subdued, outsmarted,
Now it's you who is departed.

Now it's you, who took your cuts
Of the stunning Devil's Guts
Now it's you who pays the toll
Parting with your wretched soul."

2

Joseph Robert

Bauble

I looked out and saw my daughter smiling at me from the center of the tasteful Christmas wreath. It hung above a mantel hung with stockings, stocking hand-knitted and bulging with gifts. The room was bathed in the cold orange glow of the liquid crystal display fire.

I shifted slightly to register on the wreath's motion sensor and my girl reached out a hand from the holographic display to wave at me. She looked so much older than I . . . Oh, wait. Of course. Needed to refresh. Casting my view down I saw in place of chest, legs feet the branch of a Christmas tree wrapped tightly with a string of twinkling pink lights.

Drawing from the Greater Knowledge, it was 99.5% certainty that this tree was a true, living Nordmann Fir – a marker of lower-upper class respectability for this market. Yes, this was still the old house from the listing; the angles matched. I wished I could smell the rich perfume of the pine sap I understood so well, but could never experience. This Nordmann Fir reminded me of boyhood on the Oregon coast, standing in a stiff line with my first-grade classmates before an archetypal decorated tree. A flurry of snow dancing in the tall windows behind us backlit by the weak sunlight of a December afternoon. A core document of self. Authentic heritage. This image along with a last curated holiday season playlist – featuring melancholy Bing Crosby and the roguish Pogue's Fairytale of New York – and of course a text dump of written correspondence; these were the things that drove me. My heart of hearts though was the narrative textbox completed by voice to text on my order form: "Daddy, dad . . . had a lot of pain. It was difficult for him to show he cared. But we knew he loved us . . . and Christmas."

"Sandy-girl, merry Christmas! Wakey-wakey, girlie," I shouted loud as I could, sending myself to gently rocking upon my branch.

The 3-D image of my daughter, my purchaser, my everything waved again from her wreath. Such a shame it was a simple model. Such limited interface. Quiter now, I continued, "Remember when we went tobogganing in New Hampshire? You dared me to go down that hill with the boulders, I came off and my backside was sore for a week! Sandy, you laughed and laughed."

"Jesus Christ!" a man hissed from the hall. His voice was strange, unregistered. "I told you not to put batteries in that thing."

"Yeah, yeah," said a woman, her voice matching some strands of the algorithm. There were the sounds of the couple pulling on coats and boots. "Let's go," the woman said, "We're going to run late and this rain's not going to let up."

"I meant it," the man said, "your great aunt died years ago. This is our house now."

Desperate I shouted again, "Where's my Ameilia? Was that little Ameilia all grown up? Hey, sport-oh, Merry Christmas!"

A moment of silence. Then the front door slammed closed. The Xmas lights died and the overheads switched to dim. Sandy's face and the fireplace winked out to reflective black planes. "Power saving mode activated. House secured," the soulless house drudge announced.

Ahh, it had to have been at least 5 years since I had last been awakened to this never-ending holiday season. I could check the exact date from the Greater Knowledge but, no, I willed myself not to.

The hours crept silently past until, a shadow, too small for a rat, darted across the floor, heading under the tree.

"And not a creature was stirring, eh? That right? Merry Christmas, ya filthy animal!" I screamed. That got the rodent moving again in the tree. A housecat padded in and jumped into the tree hunting after it. My branch swayed and I rotated rapidly on my swivel to see the action, but my hook lost its grip. I fell from my branch upon the hardwood floor. I heard but did not feel myself shattering around me. I had been real: I had been beautiful handblown artisanal glass, vermillion and glorious. Desperately I tried to order an emergency repair, but my outgoing communication privileges had been pulled. *Don't panic!* If I could only break the circuit from the power supply to make this end. If only I could say *F***!*, but that too was explicitly forbidden.

"Merry Christmas," I said to a brown blur of an out of focus floorboard. *2,3,5,7,11* yes, the primes would keep me sane they had to *13,17, 19* at least long enough for this battery to die. *TimestampDDLS: THIS_DAY-365.25(Current_Date).*

3

Sarah Das Gupta

Skating on Thin Ice

It had begun to snow again when Jenny alighted from the last bus. The village of Hampton was dark with all the Christmas lights switched off for the night. Should she take the long route home or risk the short cut over the fields? She was resigned to a cold walk whichever route she chose. No taxi would come out to Hampton in this type of weather. Her fellow passengers had quickly disappeared into nearby houses. Anyway, her nearest neighbours were at least three miles away from her home, Fir Tree Cottage. Jenny decided the short route was preferable. Christmas shopping always exhausted her and she was longing to snuggle down in a cosy, warm bed.

Heaving her rucksack onto her back, she set off briskly along Mill Lane.

The snow had begun to settle and had already coated the top of the bare hedges, like icing sugar. Jenny pushed her gloved hands deeper into the pockets of her fleece lined leather coat. The local playground looked surreal with the swings covered in snow and the seesaw edged with dagger-like icicles. As she passed the field at the back of the village school, she could see the dark shadows of horses, their backs to the driving snow, their heads lowered. Somewhere an owl hooted, and a lone fox barked from a distant wood. Jenny reckoned she was halfway home as she clambered over the stile into Warren Lane. She could feel the sharp-sided flints through the soles of her rubber boots, pressing painfully against her freezing feet.

Jenny paused a moment before crossing Beech Common. The moon emerged from behind banks of grim clouds. Walking was easier there. The dead grass cushioned her footsteps and the moon shone through bare branches onto the glistening snow. A few minutes walking would bring her close to the dark water of Sheep Dip Pond. Suddenly, she heard voices and laughter coming from the direction of the old pond. Local legend told how the middle was very deep. There were stories of suicides, lovers' tiffs, mysterious drownings. It was the last place you would expect to hear laughter on a snowy winter night!

Jenny couldn't go back. The thought of returning to Hampton and walking along the main road was impossible to contemplate. It was probably a group of drunken teenagers celebrating Christmas in this remote spot.

Jenny edged her way along the avenue of birches beside the water. A gap in the trees suddenly gave her a full view of the pond. Instinctively, she clapped her hand over her mouth to stifle the scream which threatened to disturb the scene. Six or seven figures were skating over the thin ice on the pond. Three at least were children who were being supported by the adult figures. One pair came close to Jenny who tried to hide behind a clump of snowy brambles. The man was skating smoothly and expertly. The young girl, her hand tightly gripped in his, seemed less confident. He was dressed in dark breeches and a fustian tunic. His skates reminded Jenny of old Victorian skates she had seen in the local museum. The girl's long, red velvet dress billowed out as she completed the circle. With one hand she clutched at her fur bonnet.

Jenny was almost in reach of the skaters. She was about to crouch down behind the brambles, when she had a view, for the first time, of their faces. The moon came out from a bank of dark clouds. Jenny froze as she stared at the empty eye sockets, the pale skin drawn so tightly over the skull that the darker outline of the bones was visible. She stared into the girl's blank face. There was no reaction, no emotion, only a whispered, comment and a spine-chilling, hollow laugh from the man. Jenny looked at their feet as they spun away. In places the ice was so thin she could see the dark water beneath. At the edges of the pond, it had begun to melt into a brown slush. Then she realised they were not skating. Their feet were floating over the ice. There was no sound of the skates, no reassuring swish as they cut into the surface. Their feet were a few inches above the fast-melting ice. Over the far side of the pond a man in breeches, a white shirt and black waistcoat was twirling and dancing with a woman in a long white dress and bright green cloak which swirled around her. The full moon was reflected on the surface, and they seemed to chase the reflection as it danced across the ice.

Jenny tried to creep away, along the path by the bushes. She couldn't move. Her feet were frozen to the spot. A force pulled her towards the edge of the water. It seemed a power, a strong, unseen arm, drawing her slowly, irresistibly. She could feel the water under her boots, hear the hollow, empty laughter. She had almost surrendered. It would be easier to slip in, to embrace the water, silver, magical, in the moonlight. She was drifting asleep, the water now over her knees. Then, suddenly the power vanished, she felt the aching cold of the water. Instinctively, she waded back to the muddy footpath. She stared at the pond where lumps of ice floated freely. The moon shone on the water, now devoid of dancers.

Jenny pushed open the iron gate of Fir Cottage. Her thoughts were in a turmoil. Had there really been skaters on Sheep Dip Pond? The ice was too thin to have borne the weight of a young child, let alone a tall man. The terrible, empty sockets seemed to stare back at her as she entered the dark hall. She switched on the lamp and electric fire in the front room.

Somehow it was colder inside, despite the bright Christmas decorations, the shining baubles on the Christmas tree and the cards on the oak mantlepiece. She flopped down into the old leather armchair by the fire. In a moment she had drifted into a troubled sleep.

***

It must have been at least an hour later that Jenny suddenly awoke. She could hear footsteps, at first on the stairs, then in the bedroom above. She sat listening. The noise had stopped. She had often heard such noises in the old cottage as the house seemed to stretch and turn in its five hundred year-long sleep.

Jenny now felt wide awake. The room was still cold as she stood with a cup of coffee, looking at the volumes in an old Victorian bookcase near the window. At last, she discovered the shabby, leather-bound book she'd been searching. She had found it the previous summer at a church Jumble Sale, while emptying a cardboard box full of knick-knacks. Jenny returned to the armchair with her coffee and the book with its gilt-edged pages. She turned a torn page with a list of contents. Her heart missed a beat, the room felt colder as she read, 'Eight Villagers Fall Through Thin Ice at Sheep Dip Pond'. Pulling a shawl tightly round her shoulders, Jenny began to read.

'In 1867 the winter in the village of Hampton had been unusually mild. There were reports of gardeners still picking roses in early November. However, the weather changed shortly before Christmas. Heavy snow fell

in the district. There were reports of farms being cut off and sheep being dug out of snow drifts. Sheep Dip Pond was said to be frozen over. Village boys were seen sliding and skating on it.

One night before Christmas, a group from Long Meadow Farm were seen skating, though the previous day the mercury had risen. Tragedy struck when a child, near the centre of the pond began sinking as the ice cracked. Two men skated out to rescue her and themselves were sucked down into the dark water. The rest of the adults formed a chain to the centre of the pond, but the combined weight was too much for the melting ice. With a crack like a cannon firing, a huge gap opened up across the pond and the would-be rescuers disappeared into its jagged, icy mouth. Two young boys died attempting to reach their drowning father. One man dragged himself to the shallow water. He only lived long enough to tell the tale before dying of pneumonia the next week in Walford Hospital.

The pond is believed to be extremely deep. The body of Marian Forster, aged nine, has never been recovered.'

Jenny put the book down. She thought about the ghostly skaters she had seen that evening. Why would they return to a scene of such loss and sorrow? What about the child, Marian Foster? Had she returned or were the spectral skaters still looking for her? In the silence Jenny heard the footsteps again. This time they seemed to be walking across her bedroom.

She walked slowly upstairs and pushed the door open. As light flooded the room, Jenny breathed freely again, the room was empty. She walked to the window to draw the heavy curtains. The moonlit scene was bright as day. In the garden the snow glittered like hundreds of tiny diamond chips.

Jenny suddenly shivered. She felt a cold draught of air. She knew someone was standing behind her. She turned quickly only to be petrified, frozen to the spot.

Surrounded by a haze of light a girl stood in front of Jenny. The skin on the arms was wrinkled and sloughed. A grey wax covered the face; the teeth were a strange, pinkish shade. Mud and strands of water weed clung to her long, blonde hair. Cuts and lacerations were scratched across her hands and arms. A wet fur bonnet hung from skeletal fingers while a sodden, red velvet dress clung to her waist.

This was the skater Jenny had seen a few hours earlier. The eyeless sockets stared, without pain, without anger, without feeling. The figure beckoned to Jenny with white, bony fingers and turned towards the stairs. Jenny felt again the power, the energy she had felt at the pond's edge. She followed the girl down the stairs, into the moonlit garden, along the footpath, towards Sheep Dip Pond.

4

Kevin MacAlan

The Plumicorn Affair

Richard Greenough was anxious to cross the road and escape the very un-Christmaslike downpour that had taken Dublin unawares. The ceaselessly streaming traffic served as a menacing obstacle between him and the monumental headquarters of Merit Equities. As Richard's heavy overcoat soaked up the deluge, he impatiently eyed Merit's impressive façade, which represented the epitome of decency in business, the venue of his next job, and shelter from the rain. Only by throwing himself precariously into the path of a green and yellow number forty-one bus did he achieve his goal.

Richard looked up before entering the lobby. The grey tower narrowed into the sky piercing ominous clouds hanging heavily above O'Connell Street. He felt a sudden chill and hastened into the building.

Richard was here because two days previously he had been asked by his business partner, David, to look at the books of the oldest division of Merit Equities. David had a brother, Jonathon, who was a director at Merit Equities, but nevertheless, it was unusual to take on a new client this close to year end. Richard had made himself available partly owing to the calibre of the business involved, but also because there was more an air of insistence than suggestion to David's request. Still, the short notice did mean Richard felt underprepared. Armed with less background than usual, he wasn't his confident self, and would have preferred that his planned Christmas shopping had occupied him this cold wet December day. His discomfort was heightened by knowing that a major figure at Merit had recently committed suicide. He also knew there were rumours that the suicide came in the face of a pending audit. Such a coincidence of events led to obvious conclusions.

And it was true. Although nobody had told Richard, Jonathon did indeed suspect fraud and had managed to postpone the audit. This was ostensively to allow a period of mourning, but in reality, it was an attempt at preventing a scandal. By investigating the matter honestly and thoroughly, but quietly and internally, Jonathon hoped to put himself in charge of the facts. He would then take whatever legitimate action was available where necessary, in advance of the audit, to minimise the damage to the company's reputation and shareholders.

David's business consultancy was the obvious choice to guarantee discretion, but it wouldn't be possible for David himself to perform the necessary investigation without raising eyebrows because the staff at Merit already knew him.

Fortunately for Jonathon, David had offered his business partner in substitution. Richard was an eminently qualified business analyst and a complete unknown to Merit staff. David had said Richard was totally prepared and more than happy to take as much time as it required getting to the bottom of the matter. And here Richard stood, impatient and dripping in the lobby.

"My name's Greenough, that's Green, O, U, G, H." He was speaking to a tall woman with plenty of red hair and even more competent calm. He imagined her CV included several years managing triage at the site of major disasters. Now she managed Merit's reception desk but evidently had kept the demeanour from her previous job. "I have an appointment with Jonathon Murphy for some time this morning. It wasn't specific I'm afraid, but he did say any time…"

"Yes Mr Greenough," she replied, quickly dispelling the notion that further explanation was necessary. "You're expected."

Richard now imagined her CV also included a few terms as a headmistress, she was quite stern, and so he was careful not to aggravate her.

"I've been asked to show you to the First Division Library, this way please." She left the desk to a lesser receptionist.

"The First Division?"

"Yes, Merit's first and oldest, the Fine Relics Trust; that is why you're here isn't it? To help with the book?"

Richard was unsure of his position, but understood the need for discretion, "Indeed," he said. "I'm a dab hand with books."

On arrival, Richard was offered a coffee, which he declined. The door was pushed open for him by his guide who then stood in the passage ushering him into the library with an outstretched arm and a smile. Richard caught her surreptitiously checking out the corridors, assuring that only she knew of his arrival. The smell of dust and leather distracted him from asking her for which diplomatic service she had previously worked.

The library was magnificent. Richard sat briefly in one of several wing-backed leather chairs grouped in clusters around low tables, but the lure of the books was too much. He was soon on his feet wandering narrow aisles beneath the tall ceiling held aloft by walls of literature, every book another brick in the wall, another step down the passage of time. Some of these books must have been fine relics themselves.

"I'm Duncan Merit."

Richard turned on his heels. Behind him in the aisle was a tall patriarchal figure. Duncan's warm smile and outstretched hand poised in greeting made a mockery of how startled Richard had been on first hearing the voice.

"You made me jump," said Richard. "I didn't hear you come in."

"Duncan Merit," repeated the man. "I was writing a book on the founding of this company by my great-grandfather and great-great-uncle. The book was for release at next year's centenary celebrations, now you're going to finish it."

"Well, actually, I'm Richard Greenough, I'm here to…"

"I know why you're here; it's a disturbing business. You'll meet Jonathon later, he'll give you his angle, but I'm here to give you some background."

"Well, thank you," Richard warmed to the offer. "To be honest, I could use some background. I hadn't even realised there was a Merit family. I thought the name was just part of the image; 'merit', as in the quality of deserving."

"Yes, and I'm a demerit!" Duncan's face wrinkled into appreciation of a joke obviously as old as himself. "Actually, the company was originally called the Fine Relics Trust. Come, sit down, we'll talk."

The two men settled into a pair of chairs in the bay of one of three huge arched windows. Richard, still damp from the morning's rain, noted the clouds had broken. Duncan sat with weak rays of sun falling onto him from behind as he faced Richard.

"So, what became of the Fine Relics Trust?" asked Richard.

"It prospered," said Duncan. "It became the core of Merit Equities, but no longer in a trading or business sense, more as a moral code. It's nothing more than an exclusive gentlemen's club really; incredibly exclusive."

"I thought I was looking for fraud?" Richard looked puzzled.

"You are, and what's more you'll find it, because I'll tell you where to look."

"In such a club? That's not very gentlemanly, is it?"

"Are you not taking this seriously?" Duncan's face hardened.

"I'm sorry," Richard recoiled. "This isn't really my territory."

"Please be patient," Duncan adjusted his sitting position as if in readiness to tell a long story.

Richard responded by leaning forward.

"Back in the beginning most adventurers were gentlemen. Hunting out Holy Grails, lost pharaohs, sepulchres, Arks and temples was just a way of passing time, a hobby. When I say the beginning, I mean ninety-nine years ago you understand, not *the* beginning. I've been around sacramental matters so long I thought I ought to qualify that."

"Of course," Richard grinned.

"Profit was rarely considered. However, about that time a few were beginning to accept fees from museums etcetera to help fund their expeditions. The Fine Relics Trust would underwrite, for the return journey only, itemised relics earmarked for select institutions. Even then, it was only to protect the adventurer against loss of revenue."

"Let me clarify this," Richard shifted his sitting position. He was still damp but no longer cold, and Duncan's manner was engaging. Richard wanted to demonstrate attentiveness. "The trust would reimburse the fees that would have been earned for lending relics which had actually been found, if, after being found, those relics were lost in transit."

"Exactly." Duncan seemed delighted with his pupil.

"And your great grandfather and his brother started it all?"

"Yes," Duncan was keen to continue. "They had both been adventurers themselves. They knew the risks, they knew most of the people, and they knew the losses. The respect they had at that time is legendary. Their motives were so obviously moral no other insurance company even competed. They built the very foundation of what is now an immense equities empire and hugely admired family business. The Fine Relics Trust is still a division of the company."

"The First Division."

"Yes. First and best; first and oldest; and 'f, i,' for fine, 'r, s,' for relics, and 't' for trust. We used to say capital 't' for capital trust."

Richard detected a note of sadness; he couldn't be sure that Duncan wasn't crying. The sun was much brighter now, and Duncan's face was virtually a silhouette.

"Can you explain what you meant by prospering into a gentlemen's club?" Richard was hooked; perhaps working on this case would be more interesting than he'd imagined. Christmas shopping could wait. Duncan oozed quality.

"This company ceased to be a family concern decades ago. You said yourself you hadn't even realised there was a Merit family. But while losing control to shareholders and boards we didn't want to lose the power of munificence. For years we'd been sponsoring archaeological digs, children's charities, the arts, opera; you name it, we gave to it. We gave as a family. Now you've probably guessed, that since about the time of the Great War, there hasn't been much call for underwriting relics…"

"You did say the Trust didn't do much trade now."

"So, we set it up as a gift fund, in the control of Merit family members, of which, for my sins, I am the last." Duncan was unquestionably shaken. His voice quivered with emotion. Richard now knew it was important to go on.

"How does this fund work?"

"Simple: Merit Equities, the company, poured money in one end, and we, the family, gave it away from the other. We also entertained, had events for the directors, provided a medical plan, a box at Lords; all the usual stuff."

"And who kept the records?" Richard could see that the full circle had been turned. This was now precisely his territory.

"The members of the club; the 'family'. Latterly, that's been only me, although they could be checked at any time. They are part of the company records."

"And have they ever been?"

"Never."

"Never?"

"Well, routinely…" Duncan was dismissive. "Obviously all the usual VAT and tax stuff is taken care of… There were no restrictions on where the money went. I could have given it to myself if I'd wanted to. The accountants would calculate and pay anything owed to the Revenue."

"So, where's the fraud? What would the audit have found?"

"Audit?"

"There was going to be an audit…"

"Forget the audit. That's Jonathon's working theory."

"Not yours?"

"We gave the word merit to the English Language…" Duncan was now weeping openly.

"So, the chap who committed suicide, he didn't have his fingers in the till?"

"No, no, no," Duncan sobbed, he took a few deep breaths. "I've been looking very closely into the First Division for my book, do you remember?"

"Yes."

"Well," Duncan composed himself. "The founders recorded it all."

"The founders? You mean your great grandfather and his brother? They kept records?"

"Yes."

"But these are nearly a hundred years old, right?"

"Yes," Duncan was now serenely calm. "Both sets."

"Two sets?!"

"One for business purposes. Routine accounts... all archived, and anyway of no legal import to the current regime."

"And the other?"

"The other are less routine. Accounts, but not financial accounts."

"You mean, like stories?"

"More journals, the truth it would seem, for family history. Though why they should want to keep records I'll never know."

"Well, aren't they interesting?" Richard quizzed.

Duncan looked hurt, as if he were annoyed at the thought of mere interest being good enough reason to open his family to scrutiny. He continued, "In the first year of our registration two very close friends of our family found a laver..."

"A laver?"

"It's basically a bowl for ablutions. This one was believed to be that used by Jesus to wash the prostitute's feet. It was lost."

"Did the Trust pay up?"

"Surely, but posthumously."

"Your family friends died? Were they killed for the laver?"

"Yes..." Duncan's stare fixed Richard. "They were killed by my great-great-uncle."

"You what?!" Richard was stunned. He was expecting a revelation; this wasn't it.

"My great grandfather and his brother murdered half a dozen people in the first two years. They sold the relics to private collectors for huge sums, while the Trust which they managed paid off relatives with pittances to compensate for lost revenues. They made a fortune and then laundered it through legitimate business. They became quite audacious... even charitably sponsoring some of the digs for items that they had identified a resale value in..."

"Incredible!" Richard struggled to take it all in.

"One such dig was for a plumicorn brooch..."

"Plumicorn?" Richard wanted to be sure of everything.

"Like an owl's ear. It was Egyptian. They sponsored the dig, underwrote it, stole it, sold it, and then had the temerity to adopt it as the family crest! It's even Merit Equities' trademark!" Duncan Merit was on his feet and moving very fast. He was agitated and angry. He started pulling books from the shelves and hurling them through the air.

Richard leapt after him. "Mr Merit!" he shouted, he couldn't help but be excited. "I still don't see how the suicide fits in."

"It's all here in one of these books, everything you need."

"This isn't really my line. If there hasn't been any fraud recently, then who topped himself? And why?"

Merit ran frantically amidst the shelves. He read the spine on one of the books then fell to his knees crying. "Four generations of respect built on murder and cheating."

"But sir, Mr Merit," Richard stood over him. "There are whole nations with that problem. The British built an empire on murder and cheating!"

"Damn you Greenough, this is what you need." Duncan Merit handed the analyst one of the older and larger books. "Finish the job Jonathon's paying you to do. Only, finish it properly."

"Mr Merit," Richard spoke very softly, he sensed he wasn't being heard and stooped to be close to the sobbing man's ear. "Duncan, why the suicide? Who cared enough to commit suicide?"

Duncan Merit wasn't listening. At first he lay on his side weeping, then the weeping ceased, and his eyes glazed. Richard ran out of the library still clutching the book he'd been given by Merit. On his way back to the reception to get help he saw a familiar face. Jonathon was walking toward him, evidently on his way to the library. Richard grabbed him.

"Richard, what on earth?" exclaimed Jonathon, rather surprised.

"You must come," pleaded Richard. "It's Duncan Merit. I think he's dead!"

"I expect so," said Jonathon, shocking Richard with his calm. "Duncan Merit committed suicide a week ago."

Richard dropped the ledger he'd been clutching since Duncan Merit had given it to him; it opened at an account of the plumicorn affair.

5

Steve Cashell

Southbound Traveller

Two women were speaking.

Firstly, Michelle's mother, who'd gone into the hallway to answer the telephone. Michelle saw her through the doorway, sitting on the floor, leaning back against the door of the under-stairs cupboard, talking into the receiver while it rested on her shoulder.

Secondly, a woman on the television. She had grey hair, spectacles and a strange voice that made each word sound like a boiled sweetie she was about to choke on. Michelle supposed she came from a faraway country. "Like many other families," the woman intoned, "we have lived through some difficult days this year…"

Deciding her accent was funny, Michelle started laughing.

Cam sat along the sofa from her, bent forward, hands on knees, his latest beer-can perched forgotten on the armrest beside him. Around his neck he'd draped his blue-white-and-red scarf, despite the room being toasty and despite Michelle's mother scolding him regularly about the scarf's scruffiness.

He turned towards her and snarled, "Would ye howd yer whist?"

His anger shocked her. Until this moment, his mood today had been the opposite of angry. During dinner, for instance, he'd gurned and grunted like a tug-of-war contestant while he pulled crackers with her. He'd clapped a hand across his chest and groaned, "Ugh! Ye got me!" when the charges cracked inside. And he'd laughed uproariously and slammed his palm against the tabletop at the jokes on the slips of paper that spilled out, jokes that even Michelle, six years old, didn't find funny.

But now, with the strange woman droning on the television and his blue-white-and-red scarf around his neck, Cam had turned nasty. She couldn't understand why. It was another mystery the adult world had baffled her with. Fuming, she looked away and vowed never to speak to him again.

The strange woman prattled on: "...Christmas is surely the right moment to try to put it behind us and to find a moment to pray for those, wherever they are, who are doing their best in all sorts of ways to make things better in 1993..."

Michelle's attention shifted to the other woman's voice, her mother's. "Aye, but what aboot *you*? Have ye had yer Christmas dinner yet? Are ye *having* Christmas dinner? Hello, son? Ye there?"

Son? Realising she was talking to Nicky, Michelle sprang off the sofa, raced into the hallway and screeched, "I want tae speak tae him!"

Her mother slumped back against the cupboard door, dazed and sad-looking. Michelle snatched the receiver off her shoulder and blurted into it, "Nicky?"

But she heard only rapid-fire pips – the sound of a telephone-box where someone had no more coins to put in the slot. To Michelle, those pips were like someone cackling cruelly.

"He ran oot o' money," sighed her mother. "An' I still havenae a scoobie how he is or what he's daeing doon south. Typical bloody Nicky. Talks a lot but never actually *says* anything."

She climbed to her feet and ambled into the living room, where the strange woman droned and Cam sat with his scarf on. Michelle heard her say to Cam, "The state o' ye."

"Shh. She's speaking."

"What's the auld troot harping on aboot?"

Cam didn't get angry this time, just indignant. "Hey, gie the poor woman a break. She's had an *annus horribilis*…"

"Ye're an anus *horribilis*."

"Her kids' marriages breaking up… Thon big fire in Windsor Castle last month…"

"Oh aye, her castle burnt doon. My heart bleeds. She'll be hameless now. She'll be on the streets, selling the *Big Issue*…"

"Selling the *Big Issue*? That's probably what *he's* daeing doon south."

Silence. Michelle followed her mother through the doorway and saw Cam looking sheepish, knowing he'd said something he shouldn't have.

Voice trembling, her mother demanded, "Who?"

"Ye ken who I mean. Him that has ye oot o' yer mind wi worry."

"I've just been speaking tae him."

"I ken ye've been speaking tae him. In a call-box, wis he?" Cam got no answer. "Aye, a call-box. Any normal person would a got a phone by now. Yin o' them mobile jobs, a Nokia, a Motorola, so ye could call him anytime ye liked. Either he's up tae something dodgy again an' disnae want ye checkin' on him. Or he cannae *afford* a phone. Meaning he's on the streets. Thir's decent folk who end up on the streets through no fault o' thir own. But him? He's probably being a waster."

More silence. Michelle suspected something bad could happen now: tears, shouting, objects being thrown. She hadn't understood much of their conversation. Again, the mysteries of the adult world fogged parts of it. But living with her mother and Cam, she sensed when bad stuff was coming.

Just then, the television caught her attention. The strange woman had vanished and there'd appeared an image of a mountain, with a ring of stars around it, and a word above it starting with letter 'P' she couldn't read. She asked, "Is that the big film?" Earlier, when Cam was being her buddy, he'd enthused to her about the big film showing on TV this afternoon.

Magically, some of the tension left the room – at least, the area of it around Cam. He slapped the sofa beside him. "Ye're right. Quick, over here!" Michelle forgot she was never going to speak to him again, hurried over and scrambled onto it. "This is a great yin. Sean Connery's in it. Playing Indiana Jones's dad!"

Her mother still seemed close to doing bad things. But Cam's sudden, guileless excitement and Michelle's arrival next to him on the sofa were drawing her back from the edge. "Come on," Cam urged. "Sean Connery, Scotland's greatest star! Best Bond ever!"

Sourly, she countered, "I prefer Roger Moore."

"Och, Connery runs rings roond him. Roond Lazenby too. An' Dalton!" His tone changed. It became desperate, pleading. "Sit doon. Join me an' yer daughter. It's *Christmas*."

"Well…" She stalked towards the kitchen. "Howd on…"

Cam whispered to Michelle, "She's been in thon kitchen the past hour an' I bet she hasnae washed a single dish. She's been swigging the auld *Beaujolais*, the fox!" He didn't comment, though, when Michelle's mother joined them on the sofa with a glass and half-full bottle of red wine. She eyed the film sceptically. "Is this all that's on? What else is showing?"

Cam held up the Christmas edition of the *TV Times*. "Just *Supergirl*. Who'd want tae watch that?" He put an arm around Michelle's small shoulders. "Especially as we have our own Supergirl. Eh?"

For a few minutes, Michelle felt happy. Christmas Day, Cam being her pal again, peace restored between him and her mother, the three of them cosy on the sofa.

But then she thought, *three* – and her happiness vanished. Three, not four. The four they would have been with Nicky.

***

Michelle left the sofa when the film became scary. The bad man sipped water from a golden goblet and started growing old. His hair became long, white and stringy. His skin wrinkled, his eyes goggled, his lips shrank back and revealed a skull's grin… Meanwhile, her mother and Cam slept. Her mother was hunched forward, wheezing over the empty glass on her lap. Cam – who, when scary things appeared on TV, usually jumped up and blocked the screen with his body so that she wouldn't get 'bad dreams' – sprawled back and snored.

She hurried from the room.

Upstairs, she tried to block the image of the bad man's crumbling face by thinking about her brother. Where was he? Down south, everyone said. Where was *that*? She clambered onto her bed and looked out of the window, wondering if south was visible from here. The streetlamps and the nearest houses' lit windows filled the bottom of the window with a yellowy glow. Above, the night-sky resembled a wizard's robe, white spangles on a sheet of black. That sky seemed to radiate coldness. She felt it through the glass. Shivering, she yanked the curtain across and dropped back onto the bed.

Something lay squashed between her and the bedcover. She reached beneath herself, prised it free and discovered a blonde-haired doll dressed in a pink tutu, white tights and ballet shoes. Nicky, she remembered, had given her this as a present. She felt guilty about crushing it and, to make amends, smoothed down its hair and held it close.

Once, her bedroom had contained many toys from Nicky: My Little Pony, Care Bears, Polly Pocket... *Had* contained them. Until the day the police arrived and one of them, a woman, took Michelle upstairs, looked through Nicky's toys and asked her lots of questions. Afterwards, most of the toys disappeared. Michelle wasn't sure who'd removed them – the police, her mother, Cam – but she was furious, so furious she forgot about Nicky himself for a time. Only later, when her rage subsided, did she realise she'd last seen Nicky a few days before the police appeared. Maybe he'd headed south then.

By the time she noticed voices murmuring through the floor, the coldness outside seemed to have penetrated the curtains and chilled the room. Also, she'd started seeing the bad man's disintegrating face again – in a far corner, inside a partly-open closet, at the other end of her bed. Not wanting to be alone anymore, she made sure Nicky's ballerina-doll was comfortably seated on the pillow and descended the stairs.

Cam still sprawled on the living-room sofa, clutching his newest beer-can. "Michelle, Ma Belle! In time for the Christmas *Eastenders*!" He opened another magazine, the Christmas *Radio Times*. "It says here: 'It's Christmas Day in Walford and *Michelle* has an unexpected visitor...' That's you! Ye're in it tonight!" But when the *Eastenders* theme-music played on the television, Cam's head rested back against the ridge of the sofa and he was snoring again.

Through the kitchen doorway, Michelle saw unwashed pots and plates heaped beside the sink. She heard her mother there, rummaging in the fridge.

She wandered to the big table where they'd eaten dinner and climbed onto a chair. Though her mother had cleared the plates, the tabletop was strewn with fragments of the crackers Cam had pulled with her: broken shiny tubes, paper hats, paper scraps with jokes on them, plastic gifts. She picked up a gift that resembled a tiny clock. Instead of two hands it had a single wobbly one and rather than twelve numbers printed around it there were four letters, N, E, S and W.

Behind her, her mother demanded, "What's that ye've found?" She'd come from the kitchen with another, full bottle of wine.

"It's a clock."

The woman smiled blearily. "It isnae, though. It's a compass. Shows ye the directions. No matter whir ye are, the needle tells ye which way is north."

"North?"

"Aye, N for north." She set the compass back on the table and manoeuvred it until the wobbly needle was pointing to the N. Then she turned in the needle's direction, towards the wall between the living room and kitchen. "So ahead o' me is north. While sideways…" She stuck her arms towards the room's end-walls. "…is east an' west. Meaning the way opposite north… is south."

Michelle was suddenly attentive. Her gaze followed her mother's hand as it flicked towards the hallway and front door.

"Now ye ken whir ye are…" She belched. "Which is mair than I dae tonight…" She tottered towards the sofa and fell into it with a crash that would have made Cam, had he been awake, quip about her needing to 'lose some o' the beef.' A minute later, she was asleep too.

Michelle took the compass and entered the hallway. There, she set it down by the front door. She returned to the living room, dragged out the chair she'd been on, positioned it next to the door, climbed onto it again and tugged the door handle.

The door open, Michelle retrieved the compass and trod out onto the path dividing the white, crusted grass in front of the house. She went past the gate, crossed the pavement and stepped onto the road. She reached the pavement on the other side, then stopped because a wall stretched before her. Uncertainly, she walked along the wall until she found herself at a corner where another street started on her left.

She crouched and placed the compass on the hard, glazed surface of the pavement. Wisps of steam escaped from her mouth and nose – cold steam, not the hot steam that gushed from the kettle in the kitchen. She concentrated on her mother's instructions. Get the needle pointing to the N. The S at the face's other end told you where south was. Pleasingly, the S aligned with this new street beside her.

She headed down the second street. Her movements slowed as the coldness crushed against her and somehow made her face burn, even though cold was the opposite of hot. She put her hands to her cheeks, worried her face was crumbling like the bad man's in the film. Above her, past the yellow streaks made by the glowing tubes of the streetlamps, the sky's immense blackness and its icy starlight made her feel colder still.

She was surprised when she found herself next to a little hut. She hadn't noticed it earlier when she'd looked along the street. Its sides were made of wood – square frames lined with horizontal boards, cracks of space separating the boards – while at its front, instead of a door, a section of sleeping bag hung like a curtain. The hut's roof wasn't much higher than she was. The sleeping-bag curtain looked stained and tatty and she didn't fancy venturing inside.

But she did, for suddenly the coldness crushed and burned her more fiercely. Frightened by the coldness, she plunged past the curtain into a dark interior. Something shifted under her, she lost her balance and fell, and her hands landed against a soft-but-thin layer that felt like cardboard. Around her was a smell that reminded her of Cam's sweaty clothes when he came home from work, though many times worse.

She heard movements in the darkness before her. Then something clicked and a beam of watery light shone against her. Behind the light, a voice croaked, "What...? What the...? *Michelle*? What are *you* daeing here?"

She knew that voice. "I came south, Nicky. I came looking for ye!"

"But... It's impossible..." Panels of cardboard scraped against the ground as a body shifted on them and sat up. The beam shifted too and gave her glimpses of what she was inside. Despite having wood on the outside, the hut's interior was cardboard. She was in a giant box. She also glimpsed Nicky's face, across from her in the gloom. It was narrower than she remembered and, along its edges, strangely sharp-looking.

And his voice had changed. It'd become slower, hoarser and – uncharacteristically – more serious. "I'm dreaming," he sighed. "Michelle, ye shouldnae be here."

"But I came an' found ye!"

"Ye cannae stay here. Not when it's like *this*. Ye need tae go back. Ye hear me? Go back!"

"I want tae be here wi you, Nicky. I dinnae want tae go back. No tae Ma an' Cam."

"Listen. Today's Christmas Day. Did ye get Christmas dinner?"

"Aye."

"What did ye get?"

"Turkey, gravy, tatties..."

"Wis it good?"

"Aye."

"Wis it delicious?"

"Delicious, aye."

"An' did ye watch TV?"

"Aye, the big film."

"I bet that wis *great*."

She nodded. "Great." Apart from the bit where the bad man grew scarily old all-of-a-sudden.

"Ma an' Cam gave ye loads o' presents this morning. Right?"

"They *didnae*! But Santa brought me stuff..."

Nicky sighed. "Well, at least they were kind enough tae let Santa intae the hoose... An' wis it *warm* thir?"

Michelle thought longingly of the toasty living room. "Aye."

"See? I've none o' them nice things here. That's why ye need tae go back tae Ma an' Cam. They care aboot ye..."

"But..."

"Och, both o' them are too fond o' the bottle. An' Cam's a pain in the arse when he jabbers on aboot Glasgow

Rangers… But they're good folk basically. Go back tae them, Michelle. Please…"

"Nicky…"

"*Please.*"

His voice sounded pained now. She had a notion that by staying here she was causing him more pain. So, reluctantly, she said, "Okay," and reached back and lifted the bottom of the sleeping-bag curtain. "Goodbye, Nicky."

"Goodbye, Michelle." The torchlight clicked off. She heard him muse in the darkness, "I'm dreaming… Or going mad… Or both…"

As she retreated along the street, she looked back. Behind her, under the yellow streaks of the streetlamps, there was no trace of the hut with Nicky in it.

***

The front door hadn't swung fully into its frame and snibbed itself. Feeling she'd done something wrong, something dangerous even, she pushed the door shut behind her and returned the chair to the living room. Her mother and Cam dozed obliviously.

She sat on the sofa between them, savouring the room's warmth like it was a huge, soft towel wrapped around her. The music accompanying the end-credits of *Eastenders* played on the television. Studying the screen, she realised that behind the words and names of the show's credits was the image of a city, a city viewed from high up in the air. A wavy blue line – a river? – ran through the middle of it.

She wondered where that city was.

Surely far away.

***

A few afternoons later, while she sat on her bed playing with the ballerina-doll, the doorbell rang and she heard her mother talking to someone on the doorstep below her window. The visitor's voice sounded like that of the policewoman who'd questioned her about Nicky's toys.

Somehow, it didn't surprise her when she heard her mother shriek, "But I didnae get a chance tae say *goodbye* to him!"

It didn't hurt Michelle quite so much, either. At least, she'd had that – a chance to say goodbye.

6

Matthew J. Richardson

The Kinmount Straight

Someone's scraped that. Look – red paint transferred to the hubcap. And…yep, a crack to the plastic as well. Must have been whilst it was sitting outside the suppliers in Stranraer. That'll be something else needing explained to the boss.

It's a busy forecourt – cars backed up onto the road and punters jingling in and out of the poster-clad glass door. Perhaps that's why the cashier hasn't activated the fuel pump. Beringed fingers gesticulating, jaw switching between gum and gossip, she eventually breaks off her conversation for long enough to glance in my direction, press a button, and point at the pump signage.

Out of order.

A shouted expletive from another pump lets me know that the cashier's inattention hasn't been saved solely for me. It's fine. Even with the fuel light on, I should have enough diesel to get to Gretna. I'll be running on fumes by then, mind.

The lug wrench is in the back, and I throw it into the passenger seat before walking towards the shop. Hopefully they'll sell hubcaps, and I can replace the smashed one on the sly. The queue is still long, but I nevertheless hold the door open for a woman with a tight bun and wearing what I'm pretty sure is called a power suit – a courtesy for which I'm not thanked.

The garage has a good motoring section – floor mats, replacement wiper blades, engine oil, bulbs, and (thankfully) hub caps. Actually, I'm not sure there is such a thing as a good motoring section – more like catnip for social lepers. I join the line, right at the back of the shop next to the groaning coffee machine.

The assistant is still holding court behind the tills. There is some issue with the foremost customer's loyalty card and judging by the forehead rubs and slumped shoulders in the queue, it has been going on for some time. The cashier is scanning the card again and again, interspersing her efforts with a set playlist of retail patter – nights are fair drawin' in noo, roads in an awfie state after that heavy snow, what's yer plans fer the weekend. Back and forth the loyalty card goes, up and down go the hands to furrowed brows and flaky scalps, jingle goes the door as another poor soul joins the never-moving line.

Sod it. I'll pick up some hub caps in Gretna as well. I push past the grim expressions and thousand-yard stares of the queue and walk into the fading light of the forecourt. The trees are already black against the darkening sky, and there is an edge to the light wind that reminds me of seafronts and nights out on the town. Fat chance of that now. Life on the road is exactly that, a bloody life sentence. It crowds out all the other lives I used to have – social, family...

Back into the familiar stale air behind the windscreen, the familiar feel of the seatbelt tight across my chest, and the familiar chunter of the engine coming to life. Needle's just in the red. Should have enough. I'm a while pulling out into the traffic – it's rush hour in Dumfries and the road is all dipped headlights and shadows behind steering wheels. Even in the short time I was waylaid, the motor has lost all of its heat. I rub my hands and wait. Finally, someone lets me out, and I head eastwards into the gathering night.

My hands are still tapping the steering wheel even as the heat starts blowing, and I stop myself from fidgeting. It's a silly superstition really, but I'd rather have done this part of the journey in the daylight. That bloody cashier. As I reach across to turn the cassette player on, I realise I've accidentally taken the hub caps from the garage without paying. There they are, still with the price tag on them, tossed onto the passenger seat on top of the lug wrench. I laugh out loud and briefly consider returning them. Sod it. That's what you get for poor customer service, hen.

The traffic has thinned out now as I head onto the A75. Skeletonised trees make a broken glass canopy over the road, itself becoming wilder as we head into the countryside. I can make out a set of red taillights ahead of me in the distance, dipping in and out of view as the road turns, rises, and falls. Behind me there is nothing – just the navy sky and the barest trace of the lights of Dumfries. No, not quite nothing. A flash – yes, there it is – of the headlights of a following car, probably heading towards the M6 and civilisation.

I press down on the accelerator. Nothing more than a tickle, really. Just don't like having glare in my rear-view mirror, that's all. You can't blame a bloke for being a bit edgy on this stretch, not with the local legends that walk it. All nonsense, of course, but in the almost-dark of a grim winter night...

There are all sorts of stories about the Kinmount Straight, between Carrutherstown and Annan. Eyeless men in top hats have been seen walking along the road, as have screaming hags running towards oncoming cars and begging for help. A bedraggled band of medieval peasants are regularly seen carrying handcarts, and a couple try to cross the road, hand-in-hand, in front of oncoming traffic. Other stories are more prosaic, laughable even. A filthy old white van is supposed to drive vehicles off the road (nothing new there, you might argue), whilst other victims have suffered the indignity of having chickens fly into their windscreens. It's amazing what I've heard in pubs and outside burger vans in Scotland.

Like I say, nonsense, although having someone tailgating you on this stretch is bound to put the willies up anyone. The lights in the rear-view mirror are closer now, rarely out of sight. Just another tickle on the accelerator, another toe dip. Need to watch that fuel gauge, though – right on the edge. I'm coming up fast on the car in front. Tourist, by the look of her. Braking unnecessarily going into corners, hugging the kerb, reliably twenty miles an hour below the speed limit. It's not even as though I can overtake – there's too many dips in the road. Too many tight corners.

In an out of Carrutherstown – a settlement only remarkable for heralding the most haunted part of the road. Nonsense though, really. The trees have thinned, set back from the road as if even they want to cringe back from the dark tarmac. It's full dark now, and the white lines are racing towards me.

This bloody idiot is right behind me now. There are times when I can't even see his numberplate. I can't see exactly what he's driving, only that it's filthy and big. I'm reminded of the urban legend of the white van. The driver is certainly large; a muscular, shouldered silhouette against the occasional lights of farms and barns as they rush by. I could really do with getting past the car in front – put some distance between this moron and me.

The car in front brakes sharply again, unnecessarily. Read the damn road! I have to brake in turn, and the vehicle behind me draws right up, filling the whole of my mirror. I won't lie –

this stretch of the A75 makes me really uneasy. The stories, and stories like them, are retold too often for it to be coincidence.

Just as I am considering a risky overtake on the car in front, the motor behind me slows and turns up some godforsaken track to the north. I catch a glimpse of a thickset man, a farmhand probably, running his hands across the steering wheel of a flatbed truck, and then darkness behind once more. Just goes to show how this stretch plays on your mind – a truck driving a bit too close and, all of a sudden, a professional driver like me starts imagining ghoulies and goblins.

One thing I'm not imagining is the diesel gauge. At some point during my game of chase, the needle has dipped onto the 'E'. All that accelerating and braking has meant that I'll not make it to Annan. I'll likely need to ditch and walk to a phone box. That'll be great, that will – a call to head office explaining how I've knackered the fuel injector.

I'm fed up explaining myself to other people. Fed up with kowtowing to a boss who's sat on his arse whilst I spend every waking hour lugging shite around the country, having become exactly the kind of social misfit who's not gone on a proper night out in years. Fed up with my wife complaining about life on the road as the thing which drove us apart, whilst pocketing the child support that this bloody awful existence gets her. Forty miles-an-hour in a sixty, hen – get a move on, for Christ's sake. I'm sick of holding doors open for people and being treated like I don't exist, of waiting in line for the simple courtesy of being able to buy some cheap-as-shit hub caps from a cashier who considers herself my social superior. Why is it that every good thing I do goes unrewarded, whilst every mistake is punished without exception. Doubtless I'll be caught on CCTV walking out of the petrol station without paying. Doubtless I'll lose my job because I've simply tried to set right someone else's mistake. Every day, surrounded by bloody idiots who can't drive, can't do their jobs right, can't look after themselves.

Case in point right ahead, as I come round the corner to see those same red taillights. This time they're one on top of the other in one of the deep, dank ditches that border the Kinmount Straight. I pull up behind her, unclip this new-fangled three-point seatbelt, and watch for a moment as the exhaust fumes from our cars roll across the tarmac. I can smell the leaded diesel from my van – probably in the last throes of combustion thanks to this silly cow. Despite the filthy state of my motor, my headlights light her up like a Christmas tree. No-one is moving inside. She's driving a red Nissan, with scrapes down the driver's side. Maybe a coincidence, maybe not. I run my hands across the passenger seat in the dark and feel the cool metal of the lug wrench. Maybe a coincidence. We'll soon fucking find out.

7

Michael P. Boettcher

What the Fire Keeps

The storm had been raging since dusk, a wild, white fury that had cut us off from the world. Inside, the air was thick with the scent of pine and drying wool and the oppressive weight of a first Christmas without Gran. My mother knelt at the hearth, her shoulders slumped, her movements heavy with a grief that felt too big for the room. In her hands, she held a single, dry splinter of oak, saved from last year. From Gran's fire.

My father stood behind her, a hand on her shoulder, his face a mask of helpless concern. My younger brother, Leo, sat cross-legged on the rug, his eyes wide and solemn, utterly captivated by the ceremony. The Yule Log, a gnarled, moss-flecked monster of a log that Dad and I had wrestled in from the woodshed, sat waiting on the iron grate.

I remained by the window, my phone held high in a futile search for a single bar of service. My friends were having a party back in the city, and the feed was probably full of light and laughter. Here, there was only the howling of the wind and the suffocating performance of tradition.

Mom touched the splinter to the carefully laid kindling. "From her fire to ours," she whispered, her voice cracking. As a tiny flame caught, she began to recite the words I had heard every Christmas of my life, but this time they sounded different, heavier.

"Oak and ash and rowan bright,
Guard this hearth throughout the night.
For the mothers come before,
Keep the winter from the door."

The "winter" felt like it was already inside. The sight of my mother's raw, unfiltered sadness made my own guilt feel like a shard of ice in my chest. It was easier to be annoyed.

Why do we have to do this? I thought, turning back to the useless screen of my phone. *It's only making it worse. Gran's gone. A fire won't change that.*

The kindling crackled, the flames licked at the massive log, and a wave of heat pushed back the room's chill. Leo sighed contented and Dad squeezed Mom's shoulder. She didn't look up. The fire was lit, but the house felt darker than ever.

Later, the pretense of celebration had dissolved. My parents, drained by the effort, had retreated to bed, leaving a quiet injunction not to let the fire go out. Leo was sprawled on the sofa, a half-eaten gingerbread man clutched in his hand, lost to the heavy sleep of childhood. I was alone with the fire and my thoughts, which kept circling back with grim persistence to last February. Gran had called, her voice thin over the phone, asking if I might come for the weekend. I'd made an excuse, a study group, a friend's birthday, some trivial lie, because a new circle of friends was pulling me into the bright, gravitational orbit of the city, and the slow, quiet world of this old house felt a universe away.

I never did make that visit.

A violent gust of wind, stronger than the rest, slammed against the house and rattled down the chimney. I flinched. The flames on the Yule Log sputtered violently, shrinking in an instant from a cheerful roar to weak, blue tongues that barely licked at the blackened bark. The room plunged into a deep, shadowy twilight, the golden warmth sucked away.

In that sudden, unnerving chill, the room felt wrong. Vast. The familiar shadows warped and deepened. My eyes darted to the far corner, by Gran's old sewing table, and I saw it. For a single, heart-stopping second, I saw the distinct, translucent silhouette of a small child in what looked like a rough-spun colonial nightshirt, huddled on the floor, knees drawn to its chest.

Before my brain could even process the impossibility, another sensation washed over me, a feeling that was not my own. It was a cold, hollow wave of *disappointment*, so potent, so achingly familiar, as if someone had whispered the feeling directly into my soul. It was the echo of my grandmother's sigh over the phone last February, a feeling so clear and external it shocked me more than the silhouette had."

"Clara?"

Leo's sleepy voice made me jump. He had sat up, rubbing his eyes. "The fire's going out."

In protest of the sudden cold, he scrambled off the sofa, grabbed the heavy iron poker, and gave the log a clumsy shove. A cascade of embers flared up. The flames caught a dry patch of bark and roared back to life, flooding the room with warmth and light once more. I blinked, and the corner was empty. The chilling feeling was gone, leaving only the hot residue of my own guilt.

"Be careful!" I snapped, my voice sharper than I intended. Leo looked at me, startled, then retreated to the safety of his blanket. I stared at the corner, my heart hammering against my ribs. A trick of the light. A shadow from the dying flames. It had to be.

An hour passed. Leo had burrowed deep into his nest of blankets, his breathing a soft, rhythmic counterpoint to the storm outside and the frantic drumming of my own heart. I couldn't bring myself to look away from the fire now. I felt a strange, primal compulsion to keep it bright, a duty I hadn't asked for but was now terrified to shirk. My phone lay forgotten on the table beside me.

The massive log, settling on the grate, shifted with a groan. A large, charred section of it broke away and crumbled into the hearth, sending up a thick cloud of ash. Once again, the flames dwindled, starved of their fuel, and the room was swallowed by shadow.

This time, the cold was immediate, a physical presence that sank into my bones. And it brought sound with it. The familiar groans of the old house were now joined by something else. A faint, dry whispering that seemed to come not from one place, but from everywhere at once—from the dark hallway that led to the bedrooms, from the ceiling beams above, from the very walls themselves. It was not one voice, but a multitude, a soft, sibilant chorus of forgotten names and half-remembered sorrows.

My eyes darted to the large, mullioned window, its glass now a black mirror reflecting the weak, glowing embers. A shadow moved across its surface, a shape that did not belong to the room. It was the tall, imposing silhouette of a man, pacing back and forth, his form indistinct but radiating a palpable, restless anger.

But it was the sight in the armchair that broke me.

In Gran's favorite wingback chair, the one she always sat in, a new shape was resolving from the gloom. It was faint, woven from shadow and memory, but undeniably her. The translucent form of my grandmother sat there, her familiar outline stooped and weary. She wasn't looking at me. Her spectral gaze was fixed on the dying fire, and her face, what I could see of it, was etched with an expression of immense, agonizing worry. It was a look of pure, concentrated strain, as if she were holding back a great weight with the last of her strength.

The sight of her spectral struggle was the catalyst. My fear shattered, replaced by a surge of desperate, protective love. I scrambled to my knees at the hearth, ignoring the chorus of whispers and the pacing shadow. I seized the old iron bellows, my hands shaking so badly I could barely hold them. I pumped, forcing air onto the embers with a frantic energy born of terror and grief.

For a moment, only ash swirled. Then a spark caught. A small, orange flame flickered to life. Then another. As the fire grew, roaring back with a sudden whoosh of heat, the room filled with warm, golden light. The whispers ceased instantly. The pacing shadow by the window vanished. And when I dared to look back at the armchair, it was empty.

I was left kneeling on the hearthstones, breathing in ragged gasps, the warmth of the roaring fire a stark contrast to the ice in my veins. The house was silent again, save for the crackle of the flames and the steady howl of the wind. But the silence was different now. Not empty. Watchful.

My grandmother's worried, spectral face was burned into my memory. The strain I had seen on her features was not the passive sorrow of a ghost; it was the active exhaustion of a sentinel at her post. The words of the family poem echoed in my mind, no longer a quaint rhyme, but a stark, literal warning.

"For the mothers come before,
Keep the winter from the door."

The "winter" wasn't the snowstorm. The "chill" wasn't the drafty windows. It was them. All of them. The colonial child. The angry, pacing man. The whispers in the walls. I could feel it now. This house was a vessel, filled with the spirits of our entire lineage, and the fire was the only thing keeping them quiet, keeping them at peace. It was a ward. A sedative. A dam holding back a sea of sorrow.

I looked at my own hands, pale in the firelight. The tradition had been passed down the matrilineal line, from mother to daughter, for centuries. This had been Gran's duty. Now it was my mother's. But Mom was drowning in her own grief, her strength sapped. The ward was weakening not because of a shifting log or a gust of wind, but because its keeper was faltering.

And one day, I realized with a jolt of terrifying, absolute clarity, this duty would fall to me. This house, this fire, this silent, waiting legion of ghosts, this was my inheritance.

A new feeling began to displace my fear. It was a strange, grim, and unfamiliar resolve. This was no longer about getting through an awkward family holiday. This was about protecting my sleeping brother, about honoring the impossible burden my grandmother had carried alone for so long, about shielding my own grieving mother.

I rose from the floor, my movements deliberate. I dragged the small, heavy oak stool from the corner and placed it directly before the hearth. I sat, taking up the vigil. I would not fail. Not tonight. My gaze fixed on the flames, and I became the warden.

The hours crept by. The storm outside reached a crescendo, a frantic, shrieking blizzard that threw itself against the old house. Inside, I kept my vigil, my entire world narrowed to the heart of the fire. I fed it small pieces of dry wood from the hearth-box, never too much to choke it, never too little to let it starve. I was a novice at this, clumsy and uncertain, but driven by a fierce, newfound purpose. The sleeping house seemed to hold its breath around me.

It happened near three in the morning, the dead hour when the world feels thin and fragile. There was a low, rumbling groan from high up in the chimney, a sound of immense weight and pressure. A cap of wet, heavy snow, accumulated over hours, must have shifted and collapsed, sealing the flue.

A massive downdraft of frigid, smoke-filled air blasted down into the hearth. It was not a gust; it was a physical blow, an icy fist that punched the life from the fire. A thick, choking plume of black smoke and grey ash billowed into the room, and the flames were instantly, utterly extinguished. The carefully tended blaze was gone, leaving only a bed of deep, faintly glowing red embers.

The ward shattered.

The effect was immediate and absolute. The temperature in the room plummeted as if a door to a frozen void had been thrown open. A profound darkness fell, a darkness so complete it felt like a heavy blanket, broken only by the weak, hellish red glow from the hearth.

And the whispers returned.

They were no longer faint. They were a cacophony, a loud, urgent chorus of spectral voices rising from every corner, from the very air itself. A chaos of sorrow, of anger, of confusion, of longing, all speaking at once. Shapes began to resolve in the oppressive gloom, no longer translucent or fleeting. They were solidifying.

The small colonial child was huddled in the corner, openly weeping, its sobs thin and reedy. The angry man was pacing furiously by the window, his form now sharp-edged and menacing. An old woman I'd never seen before was weeping silently in Gran's rocking chair, her face a mask of endless grief. And from the dark archway of the hall, they came drifting in, dozens of other figures, men, women, children, spanning centuries of dress and sorrow, their eyes fixed on the room's only living occupants: me, and my brother sleeping on the sofa.

The house was awake.

And in the center of them all, standing before the cold hearth, was the spirit of my grandmother. She was no longer just worried. Her form was flickering violently, like a candle in a gale, stretched thin and exhausted. She was trying to hold them back, a single, weary warden against a tide of restless dead. She looked directly at me, her spectral eyes filled not with reassurance, but with a desperate, silent plea for help.

The collective sorrow of the room was a physical weight, a crushing pressure that stole the air from my lungs and chilled me to the bone. The ghosts drew closer, a silent, encroaching tide of misery. On the sofa, Leo whimpered in his sleep, disturbed by the suffocating cold.

My own terror was a high, thin scream in my mind, but seeing my grandmother's spirit, flickering and struggling, transformed it. My guilt over the lost time, the missed visits, the unanswered calls, it all coalesced into a fierce, protective love. I had failed her in life. I would not fail her now. I would not let her face this alone.

Pushing through the paralyzing cold, I lunged for the hearth-box, my hands closing around a handful of dry, splintery kindling. The ghosts swirled around me, their whispers turning my blood to ice, their touch a phantom caress of absolute cold. I ignored them. My entire world, my entire being, narrowed to the faint, pulsing red glow of the embers.

I knelt before the hearth, shielding the embers with my own body as if to protect them from the spectral chill. My hands were shaking uncontrollably, but my purpose was absolute. I carefully, gently, laid the pieces of kindling across the hottest part of the coal bed.

I leaned in close, my face just inches from the hearth, and I blew.

My breath, warm and alive, was a tiny act of defiance against the crushing, ancient cold. For a tense, eternal second, nothing happened. The embers seemed to glow dimmer, threatened by the overwhelming presence of the dead. The ghosts pressed closer.

Then, a single, tiny spark danced from an ember onto a sliver of wood. A wisp of smoke curled upwards. A tiny, hesitant flame, no bigger than my thumbnail, caught, flickered, and held.

As the flame grew, a miracle happened. My grandmother's spirit, as if drawing strength from the nascent light, seemed to solidify. She raised a weary, translucent hand, not at me, but at the encroaching spirits. The ghosts nearest the fire recoiled, their forms thinning, their chorus of whispers faltering into individual, mournful sighs.

I blew again, feeding the flame, nurturing it. It grew stronger, greedily catching the rest of the kindling. As a real fire roared back to life, flooding the room with a sudden, brilliant wave of golden light and warmth, the ancestral spirits vanished. They did not fly away; they simply dissolved like smoke in a sunbeam, banished back to their slumber by the restored ward.

The last to go was my grandmother. She stood for a moment in the full, warm light of the fire, her form whole and peaceful. The exhaustion was gone from her face, a face younger and more like my mother's than I'd ever seen during these last seventeen years of her life that overlapped mine. She looked at me, and for the first time, I felt not her disappointment or her worry, but her love, a wave of warmth that had nothing to do with the fire. She gave me a single, beautiful, approving smile. Then she, too, faded, leaving only the scent of woodsmoke and peace.

I slumped to the floor, my body trembling with exhaustion and relief, my face streaked with tears and soot. I didn't move from my spot. I spent the rest of the night as the fire's keeper, its warden, diligently tending the flames.

When the first, grey light of Christmas morning filtered through the window, the fire was still burning brightly. My mother came downstairs to find me there, asleep on the rug, my head resting on the warm hearthstones... She didn't wake me. She simply looked from the roaring fire to my soot-stained, peaceful face. After a long moment, she gently draped a blanket over my shoulders and sat in my grandmother's armchair, taking up her own post to share the vigil as the sun came up.

8

Eolas Pellor

Home for Christmas

Lanny Thompson had examined every waste-paper basket in Adolphus Street School, searching for a piece of waxed-paper. He was a boarder in town and he faced a long walk to get home to his family that Christmas Eve, but waxed paper tucked into his leaky shoe might banish intruding slush and snow, and keep his foot dry. So far, he'd had no luck finding any.

As dumped the last basket he saw, in the mess of crumpled papers, a piece of WaxTite that had wrapped the Principal's lunch-time sandwich. He hoped taking something from the trash didn't count as stealing, not this close to Christmas, but he slipped his prize into his shoe. Then, his rounds complete, he took the trashcan down to the basement.

Old Joe was there, tending the incinerator; he held the door open and motioned for Lanny to dump the contents into the roaring fire. A slight backwash of smoke carried the scent of burning school work into the furnace room.

"That's the last job," Joe said. "Here you go, Lanny. Merry Christmas." The caretaker held out a small pack of Tucker's 'Champs' cigarettes to the boy. Lanny took it; there was a five cent piece tucked inside.

"Gee, thanks Joe!" Lanny said.

"Well, you been a good helper," the old, Black man said, smiling. "And Christmas only comes once a year." Lanny reached into his pocket and pulled out a card.

"I'm sorry it ain't more," Lanny said. Old Joe looked over the card which had 'Merry Christmas, 1889' printed on it. He sounded out Lanny's hand-written wishes haltingly.

"You didn't have to do that," Joe said. "But I will make sure the Missus puts it up in the best spot, when I get home."

Outside, the gas street-lamps cast their glow into the darkening atmosphere – the shortest day had passed only three nights previously and the clouds and snow deepened the evening dark. Lanny watched the snowflakes dance around the streetlights with more grace than ever a human poured into a waltz or mazurka. It had snowed all day, and the horses of the last delivery vans strained in their traces, hard-put to find traction on the road. In such weather it took less time to walk than drive on busy streets.

Lanny made his way up Jacobus Street toward the incline railway, a mile or so to the South. Joe's gift of five cents was unexpected luck; now he could take the incline up the Mountain, and avoid climbing the long stairs with all their steps. He walked quickly, avoiding both bottomless puddles and towering heaps of slush along his path.

At the top, Lanny took a last glance over smoke-wreathed Durrand, then he pulled his muffler tighter, shoved his hands into the pockets of his brown, threadbare jacket, and stepped out. The snow would make his walk much harder, but if he was lucky, he might get home before everyone turned in for the night.

The long walk to Oneida along Old Plank Road took Lanny five hours, on a good day. But today wasn't a good day; the wind picked up and the boy leaned into it. One mile passed, then two; he struggled through the snow, avoiding ruts and deep puddles that proved the planks were long gone. He was already feeling worn out.

As Lanny trudged up toward the stone church at Crenow's Corners he heard the unmistakable sound of crying on the wind. At first, he could see no one, but, as he drew near the gate, he saw a woman huddled on the church step.

Lanny knew his mother would be unhappy if he didn't do everything he could to aid someone in distress, even if home was far off, and evening closing in, so he pushed through the drifted snow of the churchyard. He found a pretty girl – only a few years older than he was, maybe 16 – sheltering against the door. Her dress and shawl seemed too thin for winter and, from the look of her, she was expecting a baby that might come at any time.

The girl didn't say much, and when she did speak, it was not English – not even the heavily accented variety spoken by Scots or Germans settlers – nor French, Lanny was pretty sure. He decided it didn't matter; the girl needed help. He did not hesitate to take off his jacket and wrap it around her. He still had his cap and muffler for warmth, and a good flannel shirt, besides.

Then Lanny assessed the situation. Mrs Tillerman's was the nearest house, just a hundred yards along the Old Plank Road, and fifty yards back from the road to the house. He decided to try there first; it couldn't delay him long, surely. He helped the girl to her feet only to realise she was also barefoot.

Lanny's sigh was lost in the wind but, without a word, he took off his shoes and slipped them on her feet. Even with a hole in the sole, they were better than nothing, though she barely seemed to notice.

"My name is Lanny. What's your name?" He repeated a few times, touching himself when he said 'Lanny', and pointing toward her when he asked for her name. At last she seemed to understand. She touched a locket around her neck.

"Bronagh," she said.

"Brona," Lanny attempted, unsure if she meant the locket or herself, but when he pointed at her the girl nodded.

"Bronagh," she repeated. At least now he knew her name.

Lanny fought his shivers as he walked, coatless and shoeless, beside her. He did not want Bronagh to feel troubled for him; his discomfort was temporary, and she had more serious problems to face. He wondered why the girl was out in the storm, without a coat or shoes. Perhaps she had no husband to care for her, or he was a brute who was given to drink, or maybe she'd been waylaid by robbers who had stolen her coat and shoes.

Neither candleglow nor woodsmoke gave evidence of inhabitants within the Tollerman's house when they arrived.

"I'm sorry, I thought someone would be here," he apologised. Bronagh nodded, and Lanny noticed how pale and faintly blue she looked. Getting her to Mr Marshall's, a half-mile farther down the road, would be hard going, if the 150 yards to the Tillerman's door had been a guide. The storm was gaining strength.

"Everything will be alright," Lanny kept telling the girl, though the truth was he was trying to convince himself.

The two struggled through the drifts and flurries. They were nearly there, when a cutter pulled by two horses came down the Marshalls' drive. Lanny called, but the wind took his words hostage, and carried them away. He waved, as horses, sleigh, and passengers turned away from them, disappearing into the spiraling snow. His companion leaned more heavily upon him.

"Don't worry, Brona" Lanny told the girl. "We can make it!" He tried to sound encouraging, but Lanny was about frozen through, and he guessed the girl was worse off. On a fair summer day, Lanny could have run the four miles to Mount Charity in about 30 minutes. But it wasn't summer, nor a fair day. It took them a good four hours to trudge the distance on the empty road.

The whirling winds drove the heavy flakes in flurries around them. The lights from the village were invisible, but the signpost at the cutoff was unmistakable, even with snow sticking to it. Lanny leaned against it, and looked at Bronagh.

"Not far now," he said, relieved. Bronagh shook her head firmly, and pointed along the sideroad that went the other way.

"But, Brona!" Lanny begged, "We can get help here. We can shelter from the cold and the snow!" It made no difference; Bronagh began to stagger down the sideroad, away from Mount Charity. Lanny cast a last, despairing look toward the sign and the refuge it promised, then hurried to catch her. He knew it was six miles down the sideroad to the next village; they could not possibly get that far.

Lanny found himself wishing that he'd stayed the night at old Joe's. A warm fire would be welcome, indeed, he thought; then he felt selfish for thinking of his own comfort.

"If only someone would come," he said. The thought was silly; who was likely to come out in such a winter storm, especially on Christmas Eve?

Bronagh stumbled, crying, her hands holding her stomach. Lanny guessed the baby was coming and, at the same moment, he caught sight of St Veronica's Church, and the deep arch under the bell tower. He guided Bronagh toward it, using his arms and hips to push through drifts of snow as tall as a man, until they were out of the storm.

Lanny did not trust the feeling that it was warmer there. He had heard the old-timers' tales about being caught in bad weather, how warmth and calm crept over someone who was freezing to death. Chilled and soaked through, his teeth chattering constantly, his feet numb, he worried that his mind was playing tricks on him.

Leaving Bronagh sitting on the bench against the wall, Lanny made his way across the churchyard toward some old cedars. Snow cascaded down on him as he pushed through their branches but, underneath, he found enough dry sticks to fill both his arms. Then he made his way back to where Bronagh sat, moaning.

With his pen knife, Lanny shaved some curls of dry wood from the sticks. He had a match in his pocket, and he lit the first stick, placing it in a spitoon he found by the door. One by one, he fed small twigs to the flames, until the fire was big enough to warm them both. The old bell tower that sheltered them was built of brick. The flickering, little fire in the brass vessel would not set fire to the whole church.

It must be past Midnight now, Lanny realised, which made it Christmas Morning. He hoped his mother would understand why he would not be there to greet his family.

"Merry Christmas," he said, warming his hands. Bronagh smiled, but Lanny knew her need was beyond his abilities; he must go back into the storm to find aid, as soon as he was a little warmer.

St Veronica's had no manse for the Canon, but someone must live nearby and, surely, they would answer his late-night knock on their doors. The worst of the teeth-chattering shivers had passed. Lanny could feel his hands, again, but his shoeless feet were still numb; he was pretty sure they were frostbitten. He put the sticks he'd gathered where Bronagh could reach, and warned her not to put too much wood into the spitoon at once, hoping she understood. Then he went back out into the storm.

At the lychgate, Lanny looked down the sideroad, hesitating. He wondered if he should risk going back to Old Plank Road; three hundred yards is no great thing, normally, but when you are exhausted and frozen, it seems daunting.

He wrapped his hands in the ends of his muffler and resolved to turn down the sideroad. Each step was won by will alone, to spite the cutting winds. Just as he began to wonder if this was what it felt like to be dead Lanny saw a house, almost beside the road. He stumbled toward the substantial door, banging on it until his strength failed.

***

He wasn't sure how long he'd been inside; long enough for the people there to wrap him in blankets, sit him in front of a fire they'd built up, and make a cup of tea to warm him, at least. He must have told them about the girl, and the baby coming, as the lady of the house – Mrs Brody – and the hired girl were busy readying a nearby room for the impending birth.

Lanny thawed beside the fire, trying to ignore the pain from the frostbite. Mrs Brody peered through the window, waiting for the men of the house to return, but when they did, it was without Bronagh.

"Well, we found everything the way you described it," said Mr Brody, handing Lanny his jacket and his shoes. "The spitoon, with the ashes of the fire, and the wood you'd gathered. We could see your footprints leading up, through the snow, and yours going away. But there was no girl there. What can you tell me about her?"

Lanny looked into the faces around him and explained how he'd found the girl sheltering – if one could call it that – by the old church at Crenow's Corners.

"Why didn't you seek help, there?" Mrs Brody asked.

"I tried, but Mrs Tillerman was out, and the Marshalls left just as we got close," Lanny replied. "When her pains started, I wanted to stop at Mount Charity, but she insisted on going past."

Half-frozen, exhausted, it was only then that Lanny realised his companion was still out in the storm.

"What happened to Brona?" There was urgency in Lanny's question, but even he noticed Mrs Brody gasp at the name, while the colour drained from Mr Brody's florid face.

"Is this some jest to you, lad?" Mr Brody sounded angry. "Coming here on this night, of all nights of the year, with such a tale, and that name?" Lanny blinked in confusion, hugging the blanket more tightly, afraid that he would soon find himself cast back into the storm.

"You old fool," said Mrs Brody. "The boy would hardly half-freeze himself for a joke, would he?" Mr Brody grudgingly admitted that seemed unlikely.

"Did you say the girl's name was Bronagh?" Mrs Brody asked, her voice seemed very old, and pained. Lanny realised he'd misheard the slight rise and catch at the end of the name, in the storm.

"That's what she told me," he said. "Her name was Bronagh."

"Did you notice anything else about her?" Mr Brody asked. Lanny thought for a moment before he answered.

"She was wearing a locket," he said. "A gold one, even though her dress and shawl were worn." The old couple hugged each other, sobbing, while the others waited for some explanation. Eventually, Mrs Brody collected herself, and fetched a good-sized cup of eggnog for them all. Mr Brody added a generous tot of rye. When he drained his cup, Mr Brody began his tale.

"Many years ago, in the Bad Time, we came from Ireland," he said. "Myself, Mrs Brody, and five children. I was fortunate to get a job digging the canals – hard work, but I was good at it. Before long I was a foreman, and I managed to save enough to buy this land."

"Our eldest was a headstrong, chit of a girl. She missed her old home, and blamed the English for our hardships and would speak only the Gaeilge to spite them. I thought her defiance made us seem like ignorant navvies off the coffin-ships."

"Well, we fought, as strong-willed people often do. If only I had listened more, things might have been different. She was only a child herself; fifteen she was." Mr Brody sobbed.

"Their fights were terrible," Mrs Brody continued the story. "Perhaps it's no surprise she turned to the neighbour's boy for love. That spring, he gave her a lovechild and, when Brody heard, he cursed Bronagh's wanton ways, and swore our door would always be closed to her – terrible words to say in anger.

"We neither saw nor heard from Bronagh all that summer. No one knew where she had gone, and by that autumn I was sure we'd never hear from her again.

"That year there was a storm on Christmas Eve, too; steady snow and whipping wind from Noon on the 24th, until the next morning. I'd never seen weather like it.

"It was midmorning when a man came from St Veronica's," said Mr Brody. "They'd found Bronagh there, frozen in the doorway, before the morning service. She was barefoot, wearing only a dress and shawl. We guessed she tried to come home, but she hadn't been able to get through the storm." Mr Brody got up and went into the parlour. He brought back an old daguerreotype.

"This was my Bronagh," he said. When it was passed to him, Lanny saw the face of the pretty girl, wearing a locket.

"But this is the girl I was helping to come here!" Lanny said, with disbelief. "The very same, I swear. I'll never forget her face."

"Bronagh was dead, long before you were even born, lad," said Mr Brody, his shoulders slumping. "You did a kindness to her wandering soul, but you could not have brought her home; my oath forbade it. I'd saved her from an Drochshaol, only to lose her to my proud, hard heart."

He lit a candle and placed it in the window, peering out into the night.

"It's a sign of welcome to the Wanderer," Mrs Brody explained as the others sipped their drinks. "At home, folk did this on Christmas Eve, remembering how the Virgin herself could find no help, no safe place to bear her babe."

Next morning, the Brodies sent word to Lanny's mother that he was safe, and they would get him to her soon, but he was in no state to travel for some days. In the end he only lost one toe to frostbite, but otherwise he was unscathed. When he graduated from eighth grade that June, Mr Brody helped Lanny to get a job. He visited them frequently, until they passed away.

Still, he never told the Brodies that, in the pocket of his jacket, he'd found a locket inscribed 'An mo Chailín' – 'For my Girl' in Gaeilge. He did not think that he could bear to renew their sorrow. When they both were laid to rest, he placed it on their tombstone.

9

Ria Cabral

The Caroler at the Gate

1

Snow fell in lazy, lopsided spirals, drifting down onto the hedgerows that flanked the long drive to Larkspur House. Holly Davies stood at the tall iron gates with her suitcase, shivering. She had not been back in seventeen years.

The house beyond the trees still looked like something from an illustration in a Victorian ghost story: gables cutting into the December sky, windows reflecting only a faint candle-glow.

Holly's brother, David, had invited her—or begged her, really. *It's our last Christmas here before it's sold. You should come back, Hol.*

She had nearly said no. But some guilt, sharpened by the season, made her board the train from London.

A shape appeared at the top of the drive. Not David.

It was a woman in a tattered shawl, holding a lantern. Her face was pale as snow, her mouth blue; as though she had been standing out in the cold too long. She raised her lantern in greeting, and when she spoke, her voice had a strange, sing-song lilt.

"*God rest ye merry, gentle friend...*"

A carol. Just one line, then silence.

Holly blinked, and the figure was gone.

She tightened her scarf and wheeled her suitcase forward. Maybe the season was already playing tricks on her.

2

David hugged her at the front steps. He looked tired, heavier than she remembered. His new girlfriend, Emily, welcomed Holly inside, flushed from the kitchen and smelling of mulled wine.

The house was exactly as she had left it, down to the crooked wreath on the banister. Their parents had died within these walls—years apart, but both gone before their time. Holly had sworn she'd never return.

And yet, here she was.

Dinner was warm, the fire cheerful. But Holly kept glancing at the frost-clouded window, where she thought she saw movement in the garden. A flicker of lantern-light.

After pudding, Emily suggested carols. She had a pretty voice, bright and modern. Holly tried to join in, but her throat closed on the words.

Because just under Emily's voice, there came another. Faint, but there: a second melody, low and mournful, following the notes like a shadow.

"Did you hear that?" Holly whispered.
"Hear what?" David frowned.
"The other voice."
But Emily only laughed, strumming her guitar again. "Maybe the house is singing with us."

3

Holly dreamed of snow pressing against the windows, piling higher and higher, until the house was buried. In the dream, someone knocked at the door, again and again, until she opened it.

The woman in the shawl stood there, skin the colour of wax, eyes like melted candle stubs. Her lips moved:

"Sing with me, Holly... sing with me in the snow..."

Holly woke gasping.

Downstairs, the clock struck three.

She went to the window. At the gates, a lantern burned. The figure waited, shoulders hunched, head tilted, as though listening.

4

The next day, she asked David about it.

"Do you remember—when we were little—Mum used to tell that story? The caroler at the gate?"

David frowned. "Yeah. Creepy old folktale. Poor girl froze to death in a snowstorm, waiting for someone to let her in. She goes from house to house now, singing for shelter."

"She used to scare us with it." Holly sipped her tea. "But last night... I saw her."

David gave her a look. "Hol. You've always been... sensitive."

"I'm not making it up."

Emily piped up cheerfully: "Well, if she wants to sing, let her sing. It's Christmas."

But later, when Holly walked past the mirror in the hall, she saw her reflection wasn't alone. Over her shoulder, faint as frost: the caroler's hollow-eyed face.

5

On Christmas Eve, the house filled with relatives: uncles, cousins, children running wild. The smell of pine and cloves covered the house's faint dampness.

They played games, poured drinks. At midnight, someone suggested they all sing outside by the tree.

They gathered, coats pulled tight, breath steaming. Voices rose: "Silent night, holy night…"

And then—another voice.

Holly froze.

It was louder now, not faint, not hidden. A woman's voice, clear and cold, threading through the harmonies with aching beauty.

Everyone stopped singing. The night rang with the sound of it—until the last note stretched and snapped into silence.

"Which one of you was that?" asked a cousin.

No one answered.

David tried to laugh it off. "Echo, maybe. The snow carries sound."

But Holly saw movement at the gate. The caroler, waiting, lantern swaying.

6

The storm came Christmas morning. By afternoon, the drifts were high against the house. The phone lines were dead.

Trapped.

Emily tried to make the best of it, serving turkey by candlelight. But the atmosphere had curdled. Every reflective surface showed a flicker of movement: lantern-glow in the glass, a figure on the stairs.

When Holly went to fetch more wood, she heard whispering in the hall.

The caroler's voice.

"You left me out in the snow, child. You left me singing, and I froze…"

The firelight guttered. Holly clutched the poker.

"I don't know you," she whispered.

The whisper grew colder. *"You do."*

7

That night, she remembered.

A different Christmas. She and David had been small. Their parents had been drunk. Someone had knocked at the door, a thin reedy voice singing.

Their father had snarled: *Ignore it. Don't let her in.*

But Holly had crept to the window. She remembered a girl outside, maybe only sixteen, wrapped in a thin shawl, singing through chattering teeth.

And Holly had been afraid. Too afraid to open the door.

The girl had sunk to her knees in the snow.

And the next morning, the road had been blocked by police. An accident, they'd said. A vagrant found frozen.

Holly had pushed the memory so deep she'd convinced herself it was just a story.

Until now.

8

The knocking started at midnight.

Boom. Boom. Boom.

Not at the door, but at the windows, at the walls, as if the whole house were being tested for weakness.

The children cried. The adults muttered.

And then came the singing.

A whole choir now, it seemed. Dozens of voices in harmony, outside in the storm, circling the house.

"Let us in, let us in, let us in from the snow…"
David shouted, "Stop it! Who's doing this?"
But Holly knew. The caroler had come to claim what had been denied her.

9

Holly went to the door.
David tried to stop her. "Don't be stupid. That's not real."
"It's real enough."
She opened the door. Snow howled in, stinging her face. The caroler stood at the threshold, shawl ragged, lantern blazing like a star.
Her mouth opened, and the song poured out, sweet and terrible, full of hunger.
Holly stepped forward. "I remember you."
The ghost's eyes lit with recognition.
"You sang," Holly whispered. "I should have answered. I should have let you in. I'm sorry."
For a moment, the figure trembled, song faltering.
Then, slowly, she reached out a hand.
Her fingers were ice.
Holly took them.

10

The others found the door open in the morning, snow blowing into the hall. Holly was gone. No footprints, no trail—just smooth white drifts, as though she had walked into the storm and vanished.
David searched for days after the thaw. Nothing.
But sometimes, on Christmas Eve, when the wind sings through the trees by Larkspur House, you can hear her voice in the carol.
Softer than the others.
Almost human.

10

Jim Newton Anderson

Snow Angel

The candles danced as the front door opened to admit the man and the child, the flickering light painted their moving shadows on the walls. The man closed the door quickly to prevent the warmth from the fire escaping and brushed snow off the shoulders of the boy before displacing it from his own clothes. He took the child's ragged coat and hung it on the stag's antler rack by the door of the oak lined hall before removing his own and shepherding the boy towards the sitting room and the fire. He sat him down on a leather armchair which almost enveloped the child and gave him a faded, red velvet comforter to warm him until the fire could remove the chill from his bones.

"Stay here and warm yourself," the man said. "I will go and prepare some hot soup, bread, and a cup of hot chocolate."

He walked back into the hall and the blonde boy could hear his footsteps echoing down the tiled floor before noises from the kitchen indicated the man was moving pots and pans.

The sitting room was slightly brighter than the hall had been, as it was illuminated by a roaring fire as well as half a dozen candelabra placed on tables, the fireplace and windowsills. It still felt dark, however, and that gloom came not from a lack of light but a feeling of chill that had nothing to do with the snow outside. Even as his body warmed, that chill entered the boy's mind.

The house was clearly that of a wealthy person. The candelabra were silver and there were expensive vases and statuettes sharing every surface on furniture that was both old and valuable. In his five years living on the streets, the boy had only glimpsed such wealth from a distance – the jewelled necklaces on the throats of ladies in carriages and in the windows of shops in whose doorways he established his makeshift sleeping quarters.

It was equally clear that the house had not been cared for. There was dust on the table and the arms of his chair, the silver was darkened with tarnish, and he could see a dark network of cobwebs framing the ceiling.

Despite the season and the enthusiasm for decoration which Prince Albert had instilled in the population, there were no signs that it was Christmas in this house. Given the man obviously lived alone, the boy had not expected stockings on the hearth, but there was not even a sprig of holly to be seen. The only touch of nature was a crystal vase on a table filled with faded and wilting flowers. He was not sure whether this deterioration was from age, lack of water, or simply because the heavy drapes on the windows looked as if they had never been opened to allow the sun in the room. The only sound, apart from the distant noises from the kitchen, was the slow ticking of a grandfather clock in the corner, measuring out the seconds of their lives.

His eyes were drawn to the large portraits which filled every wall. They were clearly all from the same family, although the clothes they wore showed the line extended backwards through several centuries. All had the same prominent nose and black hair of his host. They all seemed to be the same age – the boy guessed late 20s which was also the man's apparent age. Despite the costumes, they could all have been brothers, or even the same man engaged in some ritual dressing up game.

"I see you have noticed the portraits of my ancestors," said the man as he re-entered bearing a silver tray with soup, bread and a steaming mug upon it. "You may admire the artists, but for pity's sake do not admire the sitters. My forbears do not deserve any admiration."

"Thanks for the food and that," said the boy. "But why me? There's dozens of children living in doorways within a five minute walk of here. We passed four on our way back to the house. Why not them?"

The man cast his gaze downwards and paused for half a minute before answering. "You are right that there many other deserving youngsters I could have helped," he said. "Our age is not kind to the poor. It tends to be kind only to those who already have the most. I asked you to accompany me because you are special. You were nestled in a doorway covered in white like a snow angel."

"You're not one of those what likes little boys are you?" the boy asked. "If you want me to do anything like that, I'd rather take my chances with the snow."

"No, that is far from the case," the man said. "I have no wife or sweetheart, but that is for a very different reason. Scarce one of my female ancestors survived childbirth, and most counted that as a blessing. There is a curse on the male line of my family, but the curse on the female line is my family. Its male members, at least."

"What do you mean?"

The man was rubbing his hands together, despite the warmth from the fire. "I will tell you the story," the man said. "I am not sure if that will be a gift or a burden, but it is one I feel compelled to share anyway. It was a history known by the servants who looked after me after my parent's death, and their predecessors down the generations, but since I dispensed of their services ten years ago I have not shared it with anyone else."

Though the boy could not see the snow through the closed drapes, he could feel the cold despite the weight of the curtains, as it seeped into the room and crept under the door. The hallway had been barely above the freezing temperature outside, and only the warmth of the fire in the grate kept the chill at bay. He still believed, however, that the icy exterior conditions were not solely responsible for the chill in the room.

The light from the fire and the candles danced on the face of the man as he sat on the opposite side of the fireplace, seeming to change his expression from moment to moment as different parts of his face were illuminated. Now sad, now kind, now sinister. At least he did not always wear the stern and cruel countenance that the portraits all bore, seeming to gaze down on the boy and the man with malice and condescension. The man was only a few inches taller than the boy, who at fourteen had almost reached his full growth, and despite the malnutrition of those on the streets, he felt he should still be able to overcome his host if he attempted any attack. A story would prevent the sleep that the warmth of the fire would encourage. He nodded for the man to continue.

"As you may be able to guess from the number of portraits, the Lannigan line goes back several hundred years – the age of this house. It was built by the person who created the Lannigan Curse – Josiah Lannigan. He had made a considerable fortune in mining and the slave trade and used it to create this...monstrosity. I have not set foot in this house from the day I left home until tonight. The memories of what has happened here have seeped into the stones and poisoned every room. It was built for sin with hidden passages to spy on guests, a cellar where those captured by Josiah could be tortured and a ballroom where he staged orgies and other abominations."

"At least you had a family," the boy said. "I never knew my dad and my mum died when I was an infant. I lived with a couple for a few years but then they died too. They tried to put me in the workhouse but I ran away and I've been living rough ever since."

"I am sorry you have had a hard life," Lannigan said. "My privations may seem little to you after living on the streets, but they have taken a toll on my soul if not my body. And unlike my ancestors, those stains are not ones I have chosen to collect.

"As I said, it was Josiah Lannigan who willed the curse upon the family. He was always a cruel man – he had buried three wives, and there is evidence he also killed them, either directly or through the mental and physical tortures he made them endure. He was a master of every type of vice and degradation– an associate of the worst of the depraved who revelled in his sin. When he was 20 he had become a member of the Hellfire Club which inspired him to his greatest blasphemy. After studying the occult texts he had borrowed from the other members, he summoned the devil, and made his bargain. The devil would make him rich beyond the dreams of his peers, but on his 30th birthday he, and every subsequent male member of the Lannigan family, would be dragged down to hell."

The man paused and slumped back into his chair. He stared at the boy and his thin face and blonde hair. There was steam rising gently from his thin clothes in the fire's warmth. More and more he resembled the snow angel he had first taken him fo. Despite the horror his family history inspired in the man's heart, the teenager seemed to be taking in the story as if it were just that– a tale to wend away a winter's night.

"And so it has come to pass," Lannigan continued. "Every son of the Lannigan family has died on their 30th birthday, but not before emulating their ancestor in vice and depravity. When you know you are destined to go to hell, what does it matter how you live your life? The only convention they felt compelled to follow was to sire a son who could continue the legacy of the curse. And, like Josiah, each of those sons has been born on Christmas Day. A terrible joke by Satan to capture another lost soul on the birth of Jesus, who came to save us."

"And are you as depraved as the rest of them?" the boy asked.

"I have always tried to avoid it," Lannigan said, with a sad smile. "My mother tried to protect me from my father and at least partly succeeded with the help of some of the servants. But then she too died, like all of the Lannigan wives, at the hands of my father, although he was cunning enough to make it seem like an accident. But I had heard the stories from my mother and the servants about him and all of my ancestors, and I knew her death was by his hand.

"After she passed away, when I was about the age you are now, I tried to keep to the morals she had instilled in me. She was an angel, with blonde hair like yours. However, my insistence on following in her path rather than his infuriated my father. Perhaps he thought having a son who was not steeped in debauchery exposed his own wickedness to the light and he could not bear that comparison. Whatever the reason, on my 15th birthday he drugged me and forced me to have sex with one of the maids. Very much against her will, and, if I had been in my right mind, against my own principles. I am forever ashamed of that, for even if my mind had been clouded by narcotics, I should have been able to resist.

"Since then, I have attempted to atone for that sin by doing good works and living a blameless life. I have resisted marriage in the hope that the Lannigan Curse will end with me."

"So, is that what I am then?" the boy said. "A good work? A bit of charity? I can't say as I'm not grateful, but wouldn't you be better off helping that poor maid?"

"I tried," Lannigan said. "She had been cast out by my father and, when I left the house after his death a year later, I searched the City for her. In vain. I found out she had been put in a workhouse where she had died in childbirth. I have been sponsoring the unfortunates in workhouses all over the country ever since to try and atone, but it does not ease the pain in my heart at her passing."

The dancing shadows still moved upon the walls and the snowstorm raging outside rattled the windows with a wail that seemed the crying of the dead. The lights flickeringly illuminated the cracks in the plaster on the walls and ceiling, and the peeling paint on the portraits. The warmth from the fire stretched the wood of the floor which gave off moans and cracks as the boards expanded. When the boy and man had walked through the streets, there had been merriment on the pavements as people gave each other Christmas greetings as they passed, but the storm had driven everyone back to their own hearths and it had the streets to itself.

"I still don't understand why you chose me as the object of your charity and not another," the boy said.

"I told you I had searched for the poor maid," Lannigan said. His expression in the fire's glow hovered between a smile and sadness. "When I learned of her sad fate I started another quest. To find her son. My son, for she had been with no other before me. He had been given away to a couple who were childless – sold to them in all probability. The Beadle at the orphanage refused to release their names, and it was not until he had died that I was able to interrogate the records and track them down. They had also died when the boy was 10, and the child was taken into care once more, from whence he had run away. Luckily the couple had commissioned a cheap portrait of the boy, and I have been searching the streets for the last five years in the hope of encountering him. And tonight, I did."

He leant forward and gently touched the boy's knee. There had been others who had tried to touch him, and he had been scared, but he did not shy away from the tenderness he felt behind this gesture.

"You are my son, and although I have lain a terrible burden upon you, I had to give you warning of your fate. Tonight is my 30th birthday, and tomorrow, all I possess will be yours, including the Lannigan Curse. How you live your life is your decision to make, but I would beg you not to follow the example of your ancestors."

"What will happen to you?" the boy asked.

"At the stroke of midnight," he consulted his pocket watch, "In just less than a minute, Satan, or one of his fallen angels will appear to drag my soul to hell. I have left instructions for one of my servants to come here shortly after twelve and take you to my own home nearby where you will be cared for and provided with the best education. The Lannigan fortune is still large, despite my donations and charity work, and there will be enough for you to live in comfort for the rest of your life. The only thing I ask is that you do not have children so that the curse can end... even though I have failed to achieve that."

Lannigan fell silent, and the wind outside dropped so that the only noise was again the ticking of the clock as the hands moved towards midnight. The shadows in the room seemed to be dancing in time to the countdown.

Then, in the silence as the two gazed on each other, the chimes of midnight started to sound. As they did, the boy rose up from his seat and stood before Lannigan. At the last stroke, he transformed.

The shadows vanished as light appeared streaming from the boy's body and glowing white wings sprouted from his back, adding to the radiance filling the room. The figure's face was so bright, Lannigan could not look at it. Instead he dropped from the chair to his knees.

"You have heard my confession," he said. "I am ready for my fate."

The creature spoke in a voice which was soft and deep.

"I had no need to hear your words, for I could read your heart," it said. "You believed you could not escape death on your 30th birthday, but you knew what your ancestors did not. While death is inevitable for all humans, your destination is not. Your son will be met by your servant on his way here, and he will be waiting for you at your home. The life you laid out for him will come to pass, but he will have a father to guide him. And like you, he will be without the curse of the Lannigans on his shoulders."

The angel stepped forward and grasped Lannigan's shoulders with warm hands, lifting the man to his feet.

"We will meet again someday, but for now live your life in the best way you can," the angel said. "You have a son to raise, and more work to erase the stain of the Lannigans on the universe."

As Lannigan watched, the angel ascended, leaving him alone in the hearth. Then, after a final glance around the room, he walked back into the hall and placed his still damp coat around his shoulders. He was not sure whether to sell the house, or have it demolished, but he knew he would never set foot in it again. After the first joyful Christmas of his life, he would commission his servants to take every portrait from the walls and burn them all, as he was sure their subjects were already burning.

But for now, he had a life to lead, and his son to meet.

11

Alice Baburek

Echoes of a Lost Soul

The wintery mix fell heavy upon the faded headstone. It had been many years since anyone had visited her grave. Even the police had given up trying to solve the cold case.

Even though Margarie Wittington could no longer feel the cold, her spirit lingered as the evening air turned frigid. She could hear the Christmas carolers singing in the distance, and she wished for the life that had been brutally cut short, robbed of fulfilling her earthly dreams and living among those who loved her.

Yet here she was still wandering the deserted cemetery every evening searching for the way to eternal peace. When would her killer be brought to justice? When would her soul be released? Would it be this Christmas, or would she be passed by like so many before?

"Where…where am I?" asked a young female voice.

Margarie let out a sigh. Another soul destined to wander. There were many waiting. Waiting for their turn at redemption.

"You are…in between. A stopover before you are called." Margarie's voice was soft and light like the falling snow.

The apparition faded in and out. "I don't understand…" And before Margarie could utter another word, she was gone.

"It doesn't get easier…just more tolerable," came a male voice.

Margarie slowly turned her head. A shadowy figure lurked near a recently dug grave. The mound of dirt had hardened from the blustery snow. It would be a white Christmas.

The dark shape shifted. It was then she realized it was him. He had visited her many times in the past. Always promising a way out of the endless purgatory.

But Margarie knew there was only one way out, and it was not with him. He was known by many names. None of them were good.

"I can free you, Margarie, from this eternal damnation. Attached to a cemetery where your spirit rots. Follow me, and I can take you far away from here." His voice was low and deep.

"There is nothing you can promise me that will make me follow you. Why can't you tempt another poor soul? One that would gladly give in to your empty promises." Margarie could hear the Christmas carolers getting closer. They would pass by the cemetery singing joyful songs, just as they did this time each year.

"Hear them, Margarie? You can never sing with them, Margarie. But if you follow me, you will spend eternity doing things you have never done before. I can promise you that, Margarie." He chuckled.

"Go away! And leave my spirit be. My turn will come, and when it does, I will be worthy of it. Unlike you, who thrives off pain and misery. You consume others' desperation and feed upon their doubts and fears. I will not fall for your deceptions and fallacies."

The misshapen shadow was now at Margarie's crooked headstone. "Come with me, Margarie." A long dark tentacle slithered through the falling snow. Its slimy tip inching its way closer to her white, wispy spirit.

"You will not latch on to my inner being! I will not allow you to consume the energy I still possess. You are nothing but evil! Evil, I say! You wrench away the innocence and purity that the soul has protected. You thrive on the faults and meager sins of those who have traveled this world. Leave this cemetery…for you will not find a willing soul here. I will not allow it!"

The sinister entity contorted. "You dare defy me! If I have not you, then I shall take another!"

"No! You will not! Souls that linger here await as I do for a true and peaceful eternity. I will not let you!" Margarie used her positive energy and moved toward him, the lowest being from the underbelly of hell.

The shadowy figure darted from Margarie's advancement. It had been a long time since her inner being had felt power.

Instantly, the hellish entity vanished. He had been defeated this time. But Margarie knew he would return.

By now the wintery weather had stopped. A blanket of white covered the gloomy cemetery. Margarie stared up at the twinkling stars peeking through the drifting clouds.

Suddenly, a heavenly light shone upon her cold, cracked headstone. An overwhelming sense of transcendental peace consumed her very soul. Margarie was finally going home.

12

Hadyn Adams

The Proof of the Pudding is in the Eating

My maternal grandmother was among the last of the Victorians. She was a dramatically imposing figure even in old age. Upright, tall, independent, beautifully dressed primarily in funereal black draped with a long string of pearls, with a glorious mane of white hair that cascaded over her shoulders and waterfalled down her back she could easily have passed for a Druid high-priestess. She was well-known in the Scottish village where she had been born and still lived as a widow of six years past. She continued to assist the local undertaker in laying out the dead and she regularly visited the local sick and ailing whom she knew and who were, more often than not, much younger than her. Her

Airedale, Jock, was her constant companion and, had she been a witch, would have been regarded as her familiar. It was rumoured that she was well-versed in reading Tarot cards. No one, however, admitted to actually witnessing her doing so.

I loved my grandma, and she loved me. To me she was more than just a relative. She was living history, and she was my soulmate. When she visited us, or we visited her, she saw me as a confidante and let me into her innermost secrets. Yes, indeed she did read Tarot cards and offered to do a reading for me with her clearly well-used pack, but I respectfully declined. For one as young as me the future was to be experienced, not predicted. None-the-less she did instruct me in aspects of the art by explaining the cards themselves and the meaning of some layout configurations. She also disclosed that she could not bear to part with her dear husband's ashes, so she had kept the urn containing them in a large biscuit tin within an old, battered cardboard box out of the way on the top shelf in her larder. She smiled and winked at me when she divulged that surprise. Surprise indeed it was, no doubt about it, as I and the rest of the family were of the understanding following his cremation, she had taken them on her own to complete her personal obsequies by placing them in the family grave in eastern Scotland.

My grandma always visited us at Christmas and insisted on making the Christmas pudding. Her recipe had her special ingredient. No one, not even other family members were party to that secret which would, she said, only be revealed in her last will and testament. Of course there was one favourite ingredient that we all knew about: the silver sixpences. Despite the increasing rarity of these coins which had long since been taken out of general circulation, grandma always seemed to have a sufficient supply of them. No one ever questioned her source. These she folded in with the butter, flour, eggs, brandy, stout, raisins, currants, sultanas, mixed peel, cinnamon, nutmeg, lemon and whatever else she chose to add to her incredible, magical mix. They were naturally as much sought after as the deliciousness of the pudding itself.

Christmas was unsurprisingly the annual family gathering. Grandma, the last one standing of our grandparents, was the matriarch who, by her status and presence, presided over the festivities, her contribution being the fabulous finale of the festive feast. Mother and aunts had the lesser responsibilities of the entrée and main course. Father and uncles attended to the drinks. Well, they would, wouldn't they? We, the children, dressed the table in readiness, insisted that all had to wear the silly, paper hats, pulled the expensive crackers with our elders and betters always getting the prize together with the pathetic joke within whatever the actual outcome of the pull, and helped clear up the debris at the end. By then our elders and betters satiated from the feast were either too full, too tired or too drunk or more likely all three.

The end itself was always preceded by grandma's Christmas pudding. On the table it was baptised with brandy, lit with her deceased husband's wartime, dented, fake silver cigarette lighter. This implement, complete with a legendary back story of how it had stopped the bullet that would have ended grandpa's life, was a special family inheritance and now a treasured heirloom. The flame ignited the brandy and the pudding subsequently flamed in kaleidoscopic brilliance before being dished out with double cream to all in attendance, their spoons hovering to dig in, taste and mine for the treasures within. Scrumptious, delicious, succulent and with a most unique, subtle edge of the most delicate, crumbly crunchiness which must have come from gran's special ingredient. There was no other pudding could match it.

Alas, grandma died, aged 97, and was cremated earlier in the year, her ashes being stored in a duly labelled urn high on a shelf in our garage until time would allow them to be taken to the grave up north where all believed her husband's ashes were buried. That would be a revelation devoutly to be missed given what I knew. The longer it was put off, the better. The coming Christmas, we knew, would not be the same without her, but her pudding would live on. Come the event, however, her will had not enlightened mother and aunts, father and uncles as to the secret ingredient. The only message contained therein was as equivocal as the Delphic oracle to say the least. Being of Scottish ancestry she had written,

> "My cryptic Christmas clue now hear,
> as yees now clink yer cups tae cheer:
> If ye wad mak a proleptic puddin'
> Aw'thing that's late ye hae tae put in."

Whatever it meant could not be fathomed out, the word 'proleptic' being a major problem for all of us. Looking up its meaning didn't really help as it was agreed that grandma's use of the term seemed a kind of incongruous poetic licence. Furthermore, most ingredients of any pudding mix were 'late', or at least dried, and anything beyond those would sound unsavoury at best and positively gag-worthy at worst.

The following Christmas, mum it was who had the first attempt at replicating grandma's masterpiece. Apart from a small cache of remaining sixpences, to be eked out over the next few years, which had been discovered at gran's apartment, the result was well and truly bland. It was a Christmas pudding for sure, but that's all it was: a Christmas pudding. It might as well have been bought from Tescos or Sainsburys, minus the sixpences that is. The following year, her eldest sister gave it her best shot. Her effort gave the same result. So, it was with her younger sister the year after. We were on the point of having to accept and learn to live with failure when I, as now a precocious fifteen-year-old, offered to give it one last try the following year. I owed it to grandma, didn't I? The family hummed and hawed but finally acquiesced.

The dead never leave us. I not only remembered my lovely grandma, but I dreamt about her at times and even had imaginary conversations with her in my head. Having been the closest family member to her I was convinced I could resolve the Christmas pudding problem by thinking about the confidences we shared in order to reveal what the secret ingredient may be. It would be an interesting mind game. I was up for it!

Despite my best attempts at drilling down into my conscious and subconscious I was aware next Christmas was in the offing, and I had absolutely no solutions. I thought back to the Tarot cards. What had happened to the pack grandma had used I did not know. No good consulting parents about that as they pooh-poohed such unscientific frivolities as being typical of grandma's Victorian nonsense. I therefore managed to buy myself a pack online and looked at each card intently trying to remember what grandma had taught me about them and thereby solve the problem. There, of course, was to be found the High Priestess, aka grandma in my book. There was, to be honest, something of a striking resemblance, I had to admit. I laid her card in front of me. What was she telling me? I gazed. Nothing. No surprise there then. Slowly I placed the other cards alongside and around her, continuing to ask the same question.

Grandma's clue mentioned cups. Plenty of those in the Tarot Pack but apart from the Ace of Cups which I seemed to recall had the basic meaning of abundance, I could discern nothing that led me to any positive conclusion from those. There was also that mention of "somethin' late." Sun. Moon. Stars. All Tarot cards. Words connected with time and time passing. Early? Late? Yes, but they didn't offer up the special ingredient. There were Wands, Swords and Coins and for sure the silver sixpences were coins, and they could be termed 'late' but everyone knew about their having to be in the mix. Nothing special about them. A lot of reminders then about grandma but nothing that solved the riddle of her will. There was of course the Devil and Death. Death, a.k.a. 'late' I guessed, in the Tarot interpretation, grandma had told me, was not literal but more with regard to a transformation process. Well, the ingredients of the pudding when mixed and cooked would be transformed but that didn't specify any special constituents. I set the cards out in a circle, imitating a Ouija board alphabet arrangement in the hope grandma would actually say something to me or appear and point to the card that would give me the answer. How I longed for her to appear, to give me that answer. I was her confidante, wasn't I? How could she let me down? Surely there'd be a message? A sign? Nothing. No such luck.

I was beginning to lose faith. Then at the start of December, on a night as I lay tossing and turning in my sleepless bed, with a brain akin to a skull emptied of its consciousness, grandma came to me in a vision. There she stood before me, her deep blue eyes, her flowing white hair, her long black dress, her dangling pearl necklace. The mother, well grandmother that is, of all dream-like ghosts. Awesome. Fantastic. Fascinating. Even Jock, her dog was there, proudly standing guardian-like alongside her. Clearly, he truly was her familiar. Initially I was unnerved. It all seemed so real. However, my fear quickly subsided, for she and I being soulmates, I knew that she meant me no harm but at last had come to help me. Thank you, grandma, I intoned.

"My dearest heart," she soothingly said, "Cease your useless mind games. Abjure the Tarot cards. The answer you seek lies solely in the clue. Read it carefully. Look at the words. Understand?"

Before she vanished into thin air, I tried to look at her with an expression that acknowledged I understood. Until, that is, I realised that looking at an image in what was a transcendental dream sequence would be just as stupid as an actor on television supposedly looking at me, the viewer, and using a camera to take my photograph. Even in my somewhat hazy state I was sufficiently aware enough to realise this was a mere illusory revelation, of the same order as a dream. It was certainly not, as in the past, FaceTime with grandma on our iPhones. More's the pity! However, her message was clear.

Words. Okay. So, I would look at the words. The words Mum and Dad had told me were in her will and which I'd copied religiously into my personal notebook, in which were kept many girlhood secrets, for my eyes only.

"My cryptic Christmas clue now hear,
as yees now clink yer cups tae cheer:
If ye wad mak a proleptic puddin'
Aw'thing that's late ye hae tae put in."

I read it through. I had to look up 'proleptic' again before I read it through again. And again. And again, and again and again until... well, it wasn't exactly as if I'd cracked the Enigma code but I still had, given my personal perspective that is, a similar eureka moment. It was a cryptic clue worthy of The Times. Well, maybe not The Times exactly but certainly The Gazette, the local, provincial rag. How could I, how could we, have all been so clueless? We had been so bloody clueless. Pun intended. I got out my faithful Concise OUP dictionary and wrote down...

Cryptic a. Secret, mystical [f. LL. F. Gk kruptikos (as CRYPT, see -ic]

Crypt vault... used as a burial place.

... clink yer... pun on clinker→cinder/residue/ashes. ASHES!

Proleptic – anticipatory...

All connected with death – in grandad's, and now sadly grandma's terms, 'late' of this parish. Obvious. Well, it was now that I'd finally worked it out. So, it just had to be, hadn't it? Grandma had achieved that scrumptious, delicious, succulent, most unique, subtle edge of the most delicate, crumbly crunchiness by using a teaspoonful or maybe tablespoonful which she'd secretly brought with her of her dead husband's ashes, "something late". The ashes the family, all except me, believed were interred in a grave on Scotland's eastern seaboard. I dreaded to think where some of those ashes had been interred over the previous years.

But those ashes had in reality been in grandma's larder, in an old, battered cardboard box inside a large biscuit tin. Where were they now? After my parents and relatives following her demise had duly plundered her valuables, the house-clearance locusts had probably stripped whatever remained. The bare and a battered cardboard box, with a biscuit tin with an urn within was probably now in some landfill on Scotland's eastern seaboard. As close perhaps as it would ever get to the intended family grave no doubt. It is interesting how life has its own unique habit of working things out exactly as was wished for or not as the case may be, sometimes against seemingly unsurmountable odds.

I was left with no choice; a necessary trip to our garage.

Christmas day. The tree glittering with baubles, tinsel, coloured lights and a twinkling angel with a star on the top. The gaudy red, green and silver decorations. The holly. The mistletoe. The extravagantly wrapped presents son to be ripped open lodged under the tree. The sumptuous amounts of food and drink. The family all gathered as usual. All together in the true spirit of the season, frantically festive. And me? The chef who would do the honours of this year's Christmas pudding. One final effort. A brave, but another failed attempt perhaps? Had I in fact overread the script? Or would it this year's offering cut the mustard? (Not an appropriate phrase, I admit, but the implication is correctly as expressed.)

The chatter became slightly subdued as I brought my creation to the centre of the table. Mum poured on the brandy. Dad clicked the lighter. The pudding flamed into being to general acclaim and was subsequently dished out with accompanying double cream to the family, spoons ready to dig in to find the now very limited number of treasurers within. They started eating. And suddenly there came about a solemn silence. Mum, Dad, sister, brother, aunts, uncles, cousins paused, turned and looked at each other with a wild surprise. Scrumptious, delicious, succulent, most unique, with a subtle edge of the most delicate, crumbly crunchiness as was now there courtesy of the special ingredient. The miracle had been achieved. The hiatus over, after they had cleared their bowls, "Pease sir, we want some more," they echoed holding up their bowls in true Oliver Twist style.

Later, Mum asked me the inevitable question to which in reply I lied of course. I owed that much to grandma.

13

Evan Baughfman

The Yeti's Claw

Outside, the snow falls in endless pale sheets. People always hope for a White Christmas, but Dwight wonders if the sentiment still stands when family members who're meant to only stay for presents and eggnog can't walk to their cars, much less drive themselves back home.

But that isn't his problem. No, Dwight's having a pretty decent holiday. He's got a pair of slippers and a new robe, and his loved ones gathered around the crackling fireplace. For a bit, he was worried his older brother wouldn't make it, but thankfully Morrison arrived forty minutes ago, during the final quarter of the football game.

From the couch, Dwight looks out the window. "Lucky your plane landed in time, Morrie."

Morrison nods. "Seen worse in the Himalayas, though." He's in the recliner to Dwight's left, though he doesn't have his feet up, keeping them firmly planted to the floor.

Whitney is nuzzled into Dwight's side and is also trying to enjoy her husband's new robe. She says, "I wonder if your cab driver's still out there in this mess."

Heather, cross-legged on the carpet, adds, "The guy should be pulled over, enjoying a latte at Starbucks. Well, if he can find one that's open."

Dwight is surprised his daughter's listening to their conversation. The sixteen-year-old's practically nose-deep into her shiny, new iPhone upgrade.

"Anyone want to go first?" Morrison asks, making an effort to shift the discussion back to his earlier proposal. "Anyone have a good one to share?"

Dwight trades looks with Whitney. "You really want to share ghost stories right now, Morrie?"

"Yes."

"Seriously? On *Christmas*?" Whitney's third glass of wine is nearly empty, so her skepticism's on full display.

"Think about it," says Morrison. "'A Christmas Carol,' by Charles Dickens? Full of ghosts."

Whitney snorts. "I guess…"

Morrison also offers, "'The Raven,' by Edgar Allan Poe."

Heather says, "I read that one in class,"

"A poem, though, isn't it?" says Dwight. "And not about Christmas, from what I recall."

"It's a narrative poem." Morrison then recites a few lines. "'*Ah, distinctly I remember it was in the bleak December… And each separate dying ember wrought its ghost upon the floor… Eagerly I wished the morrow;—vainly I had sought to borrow… From my books surcease of sorrow—sorrow for the lost Lenore…*'" He makes sure to emphasize "December" and "ghost" for extra effect.

Whitney asks, "You know that off the top of your head?"

Dwight chuckles. "Of course, he does."

"Cool." Heather's eyes are still on her screen. "But telling spooky stories is, like, a Halloween thing."

"Nowadays, it is, yes. In this country." Morrison stands, moving to the fireplace, warming his hands beneath empty stockings. "But in a few other places, telling ghost stories is a Christmas tradition."

"And why's that?" his niece ponders.

"Well, it started centuries ago, long before electricity became so accessible."

"Before electronics became an every-moment distraction." Dwight doesn't like to be stern on the holidays, but he tells his daughter, "Put the phone down, okay?"

"What?" She turns to her parents. "I'm paying attention. I'm engaged."

Whitney says, "We haven't seen your uncle in years. Act like it, please."

"Fine." Heather pockets the phone in her pajama pants. "Sorry, Uncle Morrison."

"Not a problem. Listen closely, and maybe you can teach your friends a thing or two." Morrison gets back on track, adding, "Winter is when the nights are longest, right? So, to get through long stretches of darkness, people used to gather around the fire and tell stories to pass the time."

"But horror stories?" Whitney says, sipping her pinot.

"It's the perfect season for that kind of thing," Morrie explains. "For belief in the improbable, the fantastic. Whether that be religious belief or belief in Santa, in elves, and flying reindeer…"

Dwight chimes in with, "Or belief in *chupacabras*, the Mothman, and the Jersey Devil!"

Morrison smiles. "Fair. But I believe in those things all year-round."

Which is true. Morrison's always had an obsession with the unknown. Currently, he "works" as a cryptozoologist, traveling the world in search of mysterious, hidden creatures.

"Anyhow," he continues, "all that *believing* during the Christmas season thins the veil between the natural and supernatural worlds, making it easier for spirits to make their way on over here from the Other Side."

Whitney rolls her eyes. "Suuuure, it does."

Heather says, "Mom only believes in things she can, like, actually touch. Like Dad's paycheck."

Dwight and Whitney together scold, "Heather!"

Morrison laughs. "Man, I missed you guys."

Heather tells her uncle, "I mean, I can kind of *believe* it. What you're saying about ghosts. People believe in crazier things than that these days. Like that there's actually goodness in people's hearts and that good things actually come to those who wait…"

"I'm sorry…?" Morrison looks to his brother for help.

Dwight shrugs. "Teenagers…"

Whitney says, "I'm guessing boy trouble."

"Trouble with a *ghost*, actually," Heather says in a serious tone.

Morrison's ears perk up. "Is that right?"

Heather explains, "There's this guy on TikTok. We've been DM'ing for weeks. At least we *were*, until he stopped responding to my messages a few days ago. Dude's, like, totally ghosting me!"

"Oh, honey." Whitney sighs. "If he's doing that, don't give him any real estate in your brain."

"But he's cute! And he's funny! *Was* funny…"

Morrison whispers to Dwight, "'Ghost' is a verb now?"

Dwight tells him, "Yeah. Not the kind of ghost story you were hoping for, huh?"

"He might be dead," Heather says. "Hasn't posted a new video in over a week. In fact, he better be dead. It's, like, the only explanation that wouldn't completely obliterate me."

Whitney puts a hand on Heather's shoulder. "You don't actually want him dead, honey. Dead *to you*, yeah. But *dead* dead? That's morbid."

Heather shrugs. "In a coma, then."

"Brutal!" Dwight grins. "Make sure to send condolences to his family!"

"It's great that we're doing this, then," says Morrison. "Could be a nice distraction for you, Heather."

Whitney gulps the rest of her glass. "Well, I'm not really prepared for this, unfortunately. You have a good story to tell, Dwight?"

Dwight shakes his head. "I'm sure you've got something interesting cooked up, Morrie, since this was your idea? Something inspired by your globetrotting? Your monster hunting?"

Whitney suggests, "Haunted Loch Ness, perhaps?"

"Okay," says Morrison. "I've got an eerie tale that I think you might appreciate. Comes with props." He returns to the recliner. Beside it is a cheery gift bag. He hands it over to his brother. "Three little things in there, important to the story. One for each of you. Check them out."

Dwight passes the bag to Whitney. "You get first look, dear."

Whitney reaches in, pulling out tufts of red tissue paper. She then peers inside, recoiling. "God! What *are* these?"

Heather leaps to her feet. "What? Let me see!" The girl moves behind the couch and plunges her hand into the bag. She removes a skeletal, gray finger, green ribbon festively tied around its joint. "Whoa."

"That's a Yeti's claw," says her uncle.

"I get one, too?" Dwight asks, a little more excited than he was for slippers. He reaches into the bag and reveals his own ribboned claw. "A Yeti, huh? Like a big, white Bigfoot?"

Morrison furrows his brow. "Sasquatch and Yeti are actually different species, residing on different continents. What you have there is the amputated digit of a Himalayan hominid."

"Like hell it is!"

"Come on, Mom."

Whitney points at the strange gifts. "Those are tchotchkes purchased from a costume shop."

"Is she right, Morrie? You trying to pull a fast one on us?"

"Not at all. Found these at a little place in the kingdom of Bhutan. Moved them right through Customs."

Whitney groans. "Oh, I'm sure TSA loved you."

"There's really some place that sells mummified monster fingers?"

Morrison tells his niece, "Curios aren't hard to find, if your heart and mind are open to discovery."

Dwight says, "Your uncle's been collecting weird stuff since we were kids."

Morrison scoffs. "What I amass isn't any weirder than your wine collection, or your wild assortment of scented candles."

Whitney seems ready to gag. "These aren't *human* remains, are they?"

"A Yeti isn't human."

Whitney glares at her brother-in-law. "I'm sorry, but… A Yeti isn't real."

Dwight intervenes before the night is in shambles. "Whitney, please, don't—"

"What? You don't believe in this nonsense, either. I know you don't."

"Not cool, Mom."

"The only things *you* believe in are what you find online," Whitney says to Heather. "Which is its own problem, by the way."

"Hey, you said to give Uncle Morrison my respect and my attention, so I am."

"Really, it's okay," says Morrison. "I know none of you share in my beliefs. That I'm a bit of a joke to you…"

"Morrie, you're not—"

"But maybe—hopefully—your Yeti's claw will sway you closer to my side of things."

Whitney crosses her arms. "And how exactly is that supposed to happen?"

Morrison smiles. "Here's where the story comes in."

"Right, the ghost story," Whitney mocks.

"This should be good." Heather rests on the arm of the couch.

Morrison sits in the recliner again, this time hunched over, hands clasped together while he tells his tale. "My two friends and I were in this shop in Bhutan, because we'd heard the owner had procured these incredible claws."

"But not the thumb?" Whitney interrupts. "Or the pinkie?"

Dwight says, "Let him tell the story, huh? Go ahead, Morrie."

"At first, the shopkeep was reluctant to sell us each a claw, because he didn't know if we'd be able to handle the responsibility of owning such a treasure. We threw enough money his way, though, to alleviate his fears."

Whitney interrupts again. "Money makes me feel all warm and fuzzy, too."

"Thanks for working that boring job, Dad!"

"Enough, okay? Morrie, go on."

"He told us the claws were infused with magic—magic is what keeps Yetis hidden from human view. Anyhow, he said each claw could grant its owner a single wish."

"Like a little genie's lamp?" Heather wonders.

"Exactly. But one wish only. He warned us not to make any wish in haste... to really think it through before saying the wish out loud." Morrison's expression becomes grim. "Because the consequence of a poorly-planned wish could be unimaginable terror. Even death."

"Uh huh," says Whitney. "And what did you wish for?"

"That's the thing. I took the man's advice. I didn't blurt out just any old desire. My friend, John, though. He was...hungry for a cheeseburger."

Dwight interjects now. "Don't tell me he wasted a wish on a *cheeseburger!*"

"Bhutan's a beautiful, religious nation. There are rules—laws—against animal slaughter, so your diet there is pretty vegetarian. A lot of cheese, actually. Which got John hankering for his burger. So, he foolishly made his wish—"

"You're kidding!" says Dwight.

"—and was dead three days later. Seriously. When we got to Nepal, we went to Burger King—there are lots of fast-food places in Nepal—and John choked four bites into his Whopper."

Whitney smirks. "This story's a whopper…"

"The next afternoon, my friend, Gus, suddenly died, too. Lost his balance on a hike. Tumbled right off a cliff."

"No way!" Heather shouts.

Morrison solemnly nods. "He'd made his wish the day after John made his. Gus always wanted to know what it felt like to fly."

Dwight takes a deep breath. "Okay, you're pulling our legs."

Shaking his head, Morrison says, "I inherited both of their claws by default. The night after Gus's fall, my friends—their ghosts—visited me at my bedside."

Whitney narrows her gaze. "Visited you in a *dream*, maybe."

"They begged me not to make a wish. They warned me against using my claw. Unless I wanted to join them…"

Silence blankets the room. The fireplace pops.

"Spoooooky," Heather says with a giggle.

"Hold on, hold on, Morrison. You say these claws are—what?—*cursed*, and yet you're giving them to us—your family members—as Christmas presents?"

"Well, I think your claw can be used for something good," Morrison tells Whitney. "If you use it intelligently, the right way."

Heather suddenly stands tall and holds her claw high. With dramatic flair, she shouts to the ceiling, "I wish that Braeden Campbell would just stop ghosting me already!" She then shrieks, dropping the claw to the floor. "It…It moved! Wiggled in my hand, like a worm!"

"Stop," Whitney says. "No, it didn't."

"Heather…" Morrison's face is in his hands. "That wasn't what I had in mind…"

"Not the best use of a wish, honey." Holding her own claw now, Whitney asks her family, "Do you think we should see if this 'magical' thing really works or not?"

"Wait!" Morrison holds out a palm. "Don't be so hasty!"

"Whitney, come on—"

The woman raises the claw just as her daughter did. "I wish to see a real Yeti! The entire eight-foot creature. Not just its missing fingers." She yelps and drops her gift. "God... Mine moved, too!"

"See?" Heather screams. "Told you!"

Through gritted teeth, Dwight says, "Hey, you know, it's pretty cruel to make a mockery of—"

Pacing the room, Morrison says, "Did you two seriously not understand the most important parts of my story?"

Instead of answering her uncle, Heather addresses the phone buzzing in her pocket. "Oh, my God. I just got a TikTok notification. Braeden DM'ed me!"

"Right now?" Whitney gasps. "No!"

"Yes!" After reading the message, Heather's face falls. "He...He says to stop being so thirsty... That he already has a girlfriend... Oh, God, Mom... I shouldn't have given him my number. He...He..."

Dwight massages his temples. "You gave some stranger you met online your *phone number*?" He's spoken with Heather more than once about responsible online behavior.

"He's not a stranger," the girl insists. "He's Braeden Campbell." Heather weeps. "He says, since I'm, like, so desperate, he posted my number in a forum for *incels*... He says he hopes some of those creeps start calling me soon!"

Whitney holds her daughter close. "Sorry, honey. But I bet he's lying. Trying to get a rise out of you. No one's going to come calling for you, okay?"

BAM. BAM. BAM.

Someone furiously pounds against the front door.

BAM. BAM. BAM.

No, some*thing*. It growls. Roars.

"The Yeti, Whitney," says Morrison. "Your Yeti. Just like you wished for."

BAM. BAM. BAM.

"W...W...What?" Whitney stammers. "How...?

They all watch, eyes wide, as the door strains under more pounding. More growling. More roaring.

Morrison eerily whispers, "'*While I nodded, nearly napping, suddenly there came a tapping… As of someone gently rapping, rapping at my chamber door.*'"

BAM. BAM. BAM.

The entire house seems to tremble. The doorframe cracks. Splits.

"STOP THAT. GO AWAY!" Whitney shrieks, covering her ears. "Dwight, make him—it—whatever—leave!"

"Hey," Dwight shouts, shivering, taking only a single step away from the couch. "Hey, you. Stop!" It can't actually be a Yeti, can it? Has to be a coincidence."

But the coincidence continues to try to bring down the door.

Dwight finally moves over to the fireplace, taking a poker into his hands.

"Use the claw, Dad," Heather begs. "Your claw! Wish it away."

BAM. BAM. BAM.

"STOP IT, STOP!" Dwight tells the door. "Whitney, what do I do?"

"I don't know," she says. "Wish the damn thing away already."

BAM. BAM. BAM.

Wind starts to whistle through the splintered barrier.

Dwight holds his claw out like a crucifix. "I wish that the…the *Yeti* pounding on our door would stop and go back home."

The object twists in his palm. Cursing, Dwight pitches the claw against the mantel, and it ricochets right into his stocking.

Then, silence.

There's nothing furious at the door anymore. Well, except for the angry weather.

Eyes gleaming in firelight, Morrison says, "See? Now, you believe. Each one of you believes."

Whitney doesn't agree. "I don't know what just happened, but it doesn't prove—"

"My phone," Heather yells. "Someone's calling. An unknown number."

"Don't answer it," Dwight demands.

But, wiping tears away, Heather answers the call. "Whoever this is, you better lose my freaking number. I don't want anything to do with—Wait, yes. He's my... I'm his niece. My parents are right here, though. You want to talk to one of them?"

Dwight can't make out what the person is saying on the other end of the line. But he recognizes the voice as male.

Heather offers the phone to her father. "Dad, it's the police."

Whitney's confused. "The police?"

"They said they tried calling you guys, but you don't have your phones with you."

Heart hammering, Dwight takes the phone and speaks into it. "Hi, this is Dwight..."

"Yes, hello," the voice says. "Sir, my name is Lieutenant Meggins. Sorry to bother you this evening. But are you the brother of Morrison Jacobs?"

"Yeah, he's my brother..."

"I'm sorry, Mr. Jacobs, to inform you that there's been an accident. A car accident, sir, involving your brother."

"I'm sorry, *what*? That's not possible..."

"We need you to please come down to the hospital, and—"

"That can't be right..." says Dwight, forcing an awkward grin. "I *know* it's not right. I mean, Morrie's standing right here in front of me."

"Morrison's here at the hospital, Mr. Jacobs, and we need you to—"

"No..." Dwight shudders. "That...That can't *be!*"

Lieutenant Meggins shares more details with Dwight. Dwight's jaw drops.

"I did eventually make my wish," Morrison says, standing with his back to the others, staring into dancing flames. "Recently, I wished that my family would finally believe in what I believe—the improbable, the fantastic—at no matter the cost to me. And this... Well, this—tonight—is the result."

Dwight tries passing the phone to his brother. "Talk to this guy, Morrie. There's been some sort of mix-up. He says your taxi... That you *were in a car crash* just outside the airport... It's ridiculous. Here, Morrie, take the phone. Morrie...?"

Morrison ignores the phone. "You said you didn't have a ghost story to tell? Well, guess what? Now you do..."

He turns to his family, his face now mangled, his eyes red and leaking, his neck snapped at a gruesome angle. "Boo!"

14

Plamen Vasilev

The Holly King's Curse

Snow fell in slow spirals, veiling the sleepy English countryside under a silver hush. On the edge of the small village of Hartwick stood Gravesend Manor, an ancient house whose chimneys rarely smoked and whose windows reflected only the shadows of passing crows. For as long as the villagers remembered, the estate had been abandoned during the Yuletide season. Rumor had it that no family ever lasted through a Christmas night within its walls.

This year, however, the manor was to receive guests once more.

The Return

Dr. Clara Henshaw, a historian from Cambridge, arrived in Hartwick on a frosted December afternoon with her companion, Daniel Whitaker, a playwright who had recently fallen out of favor in London. They had been invited by the new owner of the manor, Sir Edmund Ravel, a reclusive philanthropist with eccentric tastes.

Their carriage jolted to a halt before the towering gates of Gravesend. Ivy strangled the stone walls, and an ancient holly tree bent crookedly at the entrance, its berries gleaming like drops of blood.

Clara tugged her scarf tighter.

Clara: "They say the holly tree marks where the last master of the house was buried. Without a coffin."

Daniel: "And here I thought you invited me for Christmas cheer, not ghost stories."

The gates creaked open as if of their own accord.

Part I: The Feast

Inside, the manor was unexpectedly warm. Candlelight flickered from brass sconces, garlands of holly and pine were draped across staircases, and a roaring fire filled the great hall with golden light. At the far end stood Sir Edmund, tall and pale, his gray hair swept back like wings. His smile was warm but strained, as if practiced before a mirror.

Sir Edmund: "Welcome, my friends. Tonight we break a tradition of silence. Gravesend has been dark for too many winters. This Christmas, it shall live again."

A long oak table was laid with roasted goose, sugared plums, and steaming bowls of wassail. Clara felt the historian in her stir with fascination. Every ornament seemed rooted in medieval custom—the candles in the windows, the carved wooden yule log burning on the hearth, even the ivy crowns resting on their chairs.

Daniel raised his glass.

Daniel: "To new beginnings—and to old houses that pretend to be hospitable."

His attempt at humor drew a brittle laugh from Sir Edmund.

But as they feasted, Clara noticed something strange: the holly berries in the garlands had begun to blacken, their glossy red skins shriveling to ash. No one else seemed to see it.

Part II: The Carolers

Later that evening, music drifted faintly through the hall. Not the bright cheer of carolers, but a thin, mournful chant, half a hymn and half a dirge. Daniel frowned and pressed his ear to the frost-streaked window.

Outside stood a procession of figures cloaked in snow and shadow, their faces hidden beneath wreaths of holly. They did not move, save for their lips, which murmured the same line again and again:

"The Holly King must reign... until the bloodline ends."

Clara shivered.

Clara: "What bloodline?"

Sir Edmund (suddenly sharp): "Nothing you need concern yourself with. Superstitious villagers. Pay them no mind."

But when Clara looked again, the carolers were gone, leaving only deep footprints in the snow that led toward the crooked holly tree at the gate.

Part III: The Tale of Gravesend

That night, Sir Edmund insisted they sit by the fire for a toast. He poured them mulled wine, though he barely touched his own cup.

Clara, ever the scholar, pressed him for the manor's history. At first, he resisted, but under Daniel's teasing persistence, he relented.

Sir Edmund: "Very well. The legend is as old as winter itself. Once, centuries ago, this land was ruled not by kings, but by two spirits—the Oak King and the Holly King. The Oak ruled the light half of the year, from midsummer to midwinter. Holly ruled the dark half. Each solstice, one slew the other, only to be reborn when his season came again."

The fire hissed as sap cracked in the log.

Sir Edmund: "The Holly King demanded tribute in blood. One of my ancestors defied him, refusing the sacrifice. The story claims the Holy King cursed our line—that each Yuletide, one of us would die within these walls, until the family tree was barren."

Clara's scholar's mind whirred. The holy wreaths, the chants outside, the blackening berries—everything pointed to a ritual still alive.

Daniel, less impressed, chuckled nervously.

Daniel: "So you invited us here for Christmas… or for company to die with?"

Sir Edmund's eyes flashed with something between sorrow and terror.

Sir Edmund: "I invited you because I do not wish to be alone when he comes."

Part IV: Midnight Whispers

Near midnight, Clara was woken by a sound like whispering leaves. Rising, she wandered into the corridor, where shadows moved as if stirred by a hidden breeze.

The garlands of holly along the walls had withered to brittle husks, their berries fallen and crushed beneath invisible feet. From the drawing room, she heard Daniel's voice.

When she entered, she found him staring into a cracked mirror.

Daniel: "Clara, look… it shows me older. Decades older. My hair gray, my skin like his."

The mirror shimmered. Behind Daniel's reflection stood a figure crowned in holly, its eyes pits of coal, its mouth dripping shadow. When Clara blinked, it was gone.

Clara: "This house is feeding us to something. The curse isn't just his family—it's anyone who stays."

From the fireplace, ashes stirred into the air, forming words against the stone:

"The Holly King will have his due."

Part V: The Yule Log

The next evening, Sir Edmund insisted they all gather again in the great hall. He seemed frail now, his skin as pale as candle wax. The yule log on the hearth burned low, its flames crawling as if reluctant to give light.

Suddenly, the chanting began again outside. This time, it was louder—dozens of voices rising in cold harmony. Clara dared to look through the window. The carolers had returned, but their faces were not hidden. They were corpses, their lips blue, their eyes rolled back white, yet their mouths still moved.

Daniel swore under his breath.

Daniel: "They're not villagers."

Clara: "They're his ancestors."

Sir Edmund dropped to his knees.

Sir Edmund: "It is too late. The Holy King has come to claim me."

The front doors thundered open, though no wind entered. Instead, the holy garlands writhed like serpents, lashing toward the hearth. The yule log split, releasing a stench of rot. From its embers rose a towering figure draped in leaves, its antlered crown scraping the ceiling—the Holly King incarnate.

Part VI: The Bargain

The Holly King's voice was like branches snapping under snow.

Holly King: "The blood of Ravel is mine. I will not be denied."

Sir Edmund, trembling, crawled forward

Sir Edmund: "Then take me, and spare the others!"

But Clara stepped between them.

Clara: "Wait. The stories say you and the Oak King trade places. Your reign must end in midwinter. That's the law of the solstice."

The King's shadowy face twisted.

Holly King: "Unless the tribute binds me. Unless the line feeds me. Then my reign is eternal."

Daniel, pale but defiant, spat into the fire.

Daniel: "You're just another parasite. No crown, no kingdom—just a weed choking the roots."

The Holly King reached for him, but Clara thrust a candle into the garland on the mantle. The dry holly burst into flame, catching across the hall. The King roared, recoiling.

Clara: "Burn the holly! That's his tether."

Part VII: The Last Sacrifice

Flames devoured the garlands, filling the hall with smoke and sparks. The ghostly carolers wailed from outside, their voices unraveling. Yet the King still loomed, his crown blazing but unbroken.

Sir Edmund staggered to his feet.

Sir Edmund: "The curse began with my ancestor's defiance. Let it end with mine. If my death severs the bloodline, he cannot return."

Clara reached for him, but he smiled with weary resolve.

Sir Edmund: "Christmas is sacrifice, is it not? One life for many."

Before they could stop him, Edmund threw himself into the burning hearth. His body vanished in the blaze, and with a scream like winter itself, the Holly King burst into ash.

The carolers outside collapsed into snowdrifts. The manor shook, then fell silent.

The Morning After

When dawn came, the fire had burned out, leaving only cinders. Clara and Daniel stumbled into the snow, coughing, their clothes reeking of smoke. The holly tree at the gate had withered to blackened bark.

They never found Edmund's body.

For years afterward, Gravesend Manor stood empty. Yet every Christmas Eve, villagers claimed they saw a single figure in the window, watching over the hearth. Not the Holly King, but Edmund himself, guarding the world from the curse he had carried.

And sometimes, when the snow fell deepest, a faint voice could still be heard among the drifting carols:

"The Holly King must reign… until the bloodline ends."

15

Monti Sturzaker

The Wine Coloured Dress

She came in a wine-coloured dress at Christmas. I glanced up for a second, over the crisp skin of the turkey, through the frosted window, past the clothesline into the park and saw her. She sat on the swing, motionless. For a second, I thought I had hallucinated her but there she stayed and I stood — how could I not — and left the house straight away. Shoeless, crunching across the snow, hatless, coatless, gloveless. How strange a playground seems in winter, wind whistling through the deserted swings, frost glistening on the slide. She stood to address me as if nothing was disparate, as if she hadn't died, as if her standing here was exactly what I should have anticipated.

"Hello," she said, her voice sultry like I remembered.

"Alyssa," I spoke, a tremor on the end of the 'A', a whistle of breath on the 'S'. She smiled and hugged me, her unspoiled body frozen and soft as if she were not cumulonimbus constructed solely from the fragments of my memories. I shivered.

"Am I dreaming?" I asked. She released me, shaking her head.

"Why did I die?" — not accusatory. A pause, an escape of the conversation's breath, a sigh, a gasp, a wheeze. It conceded permission for the question to go unanswered. To be unanswerable.

"Are you staying?" we had always been like this, responses in the blink of an eye or the squeeze of one's shoulders.

"Alas," she whispered, superfluous.

"Come in, at least, out of the cold," — uncertain. She laughed, silvery locks spilling over her shoulders. She looked as beautiful as ever; my breath caught for a split second.

"Go," she insisted, and disappeared.

***

She came in a wine-coloured dress at Christmas. She was an expected and asked-for guest. I hadn't busied myself with the traditions — how could I — they seemed a waste; I sat instead on the relinquished swings anticipating her arrival. It wasn't so much an approach as a materialisation. One second she was not, the next she was, her feet a pendulous invitation beside me.

"Hello," she said, sounding as if no time at all had passed, the year before naught but a hazy fantasy.

"Alyssa." Perfunctory, it would seem, but I said it nonetheless, feeling the softness of the 'S', the slide of the 'L' against my lips.

"News?" she asked, but I had none in the slightest. The years seemed pointless now, without her. My days oozed slowly, sand in an endless timer, spilling over and over until I would have another second with her, another minute, another hour. Until I could see her face and hear her voice once more. The cold steel of the swingset seemed to masticate my flesh; the most alive I'd felt since she died, the wind stinging against my cheeks. I shivered.

"Do you miss me?" The question I'd been expecting materialising in a breathy husk. The wind whirled around us: my teeth clenching against it, her unmolested. I wished it had blown her dress at least, so I could be sure I wasn't fantasising.

"I do," I reassured her. I did. So why did it feel like a fiction?

"You do," she promised, vanishing.

***

She came in a wine-coloured dress at Christmas. I knew she would come, and yet I loitered in the warmth of the kitchen. The playground was never as alive as when she was present in it, yet it was never as dead either. Despite my best intentions, I found myself slipping layers on, preserving the warmth — and the distance — for as long as possible. She waited, patient as always, until I, sighing, shuffled down through the snow. I paused by the slide, icy.

"You wish for me to leave?" she asked.

"Yes," I spat. So many falsehoods. She smiled, caressing the shadowed seat beside her until I reluctantly sat. We waited in silence, an intermission only I could conclude. She had this way of seducing the truth out of me.

"You've destroyed Christmas for me enough now," I huffed, my breath a small cirrostratus. Nonchalant, she smoothed her dress, hands pale against the rich crimson red.

"Do you regret it?" I asked. She held my gaze, hers lapis lazuli. We shared a reminiscence from contrasting angles, mine of her, coming in a wine-coloured dress, her hands pressed against his chest. Hers of him, indisputably, of my face as I caught them together. Did she picture her dress white or was the wine as persistent in her memory as it was in mine?

"I do," she said, showing me that she could lie too. "Do you?"

That Christmas, she came in a snow-white dress. She'd brought dessert, burdensome in her small hands. She let herself in. My brother was here already, assisting me with the turkey, whisky on his breath and in his head. They exchanged a kiss, a pleasantry but nothing else. Acquaintances with a shared association.

I watched them conduct themselves as friends, all while knowing as I did, what I knew about them. What I'd seen in the texts. Later, giddy from wine, whisky and food, I left them alone together, stepping out for a cigarette into the whistling Christmas night. Sitting on the swings, I looked in, past the clothesline, through the frosted window, over the drying china and chanced to glimpse her — glimpse them. I stood — how could I not — and before I realised what I was doing I had fished turkey knife from sink. I remember his hands on her white thighs, their shared expression, the wine stain spreading across the snow of her dress. Mostly, I remember her eyes, bleached blue and cold as ice. The earth was so dense, but I slashed at it until it made space for them both to lie in a lover's eternal embrace beneath the swings — and, just as soon as she had been, she was gone.

***

"Do you?" she asked once more, but even the sweetest-tasting lie would've felt a falsehood from my lips.

16

Subham Rai

The Holly Locket Curse

Theodore Whitaker, a curator buried in relics' dust, felt Christmas Eve 2025 creep like frost over his Bindweed Path cottage, its stone walls snared by snow-draped vines. The village beyond glittered with drone-lit carols, their synthetic hum piercing the night's hush, but Theo, forty-six, sought refuge in his parlor's dim hearth. His lean frame moved with care, spectacles slipping down a nose sharpened by years unraveling ancient scripts. The world outside pulsed with festive cheer, its lights twinkling through the haze, yet the cottage, inherited from distant Hargrave kin, stood apart, its overgrown path a barrier to holiday clamor.

Lydia's loss haunted Theo more than his museum tomes. Five winters ago, her illness stole their holiday warmth, her laughter over garlands and gentle touch at midnight toasts fading into memory. Solitude now cloaked him, heavier than the snow piling against frosted panes. Tonight, an odd urge, sharp as a splinter, drew him to an auction crate, its wood scarred by careless hands. He pried it open, the hinges groaning like a distant wail, releasing a musty scent that mingled with the hearth's faint pine. Among faded letters, brittle as old bones, and tarnished trinkets lay a silver locket, its holly etchings catching the firelight in delicate glints. A yellowed note slipped free, its Victorian script stark: Holly curse stirs frost kin.

Theo's lips twitched, a faint chuckle breaking the silence. "Mere folklore," he muttered, setting the locket beside a pine bough on the mantel, his only nod to festivity. Yet Lydia's memory surged, her tales of Hargrave kin, their relics steeped in shadow, echoing the note's cryptic warning. The cottage, a Hargrave heirloom, felt heavier, its vine-choked walls pressing inward, as if guarding secrets older than its stones. Vines scraped frosted panes, their rustle weaving dread into the hearth's flicker, a subtle challenge to the season's forced joy.

He paced, stirring dust on threadbare rugs, the grandfather clock's ticks sharpening his thoughts. Curiosity, his lifelong guide, flared. Had he not cracked stranger riddles in dusty archives, piecing together fragments of forgotten lives? Lydia's voice lingered, her teasing about his bookish heart stirring a romantic ache, a longing for their shared evenings by the fire. The locket's weight in his palm felt alive, whispering secrets he could almost grasp. "Calling spirits, now?" he jested, his voice low, yet the vines' insistent scratch carried a chilling edge, tainting the solstice hush.

Theo turned the locket over, its holly etchings sharp under his thumb, their intricate leaves seeming to shift in the firelight. The note's warning, Holly curse stirs frost kin, looped in his mind, tying to Lydia's stories of Hargrave ancestors who dabbled in forbidden lore. He recalled her final Christmas, her frail hands tracing a family brooch, her voice soft with tales of their quirks, their relics hinting at unseen debts. That memory hollowed him, the holiday's cheer a mockery of his loss. The cottage, once a scholarly haven, now felt like a cage, its vines mirroring an inner snare he could not name.

He set the locket down, then retrieved it, unable to resist its pull. The clock's ticks grew louder, each one a prod to his curiosity, urging him to test the relic's promise. What harm in a trinket's secret? A wry smile crossed his face at the absurdity, yet the vines' rustle deepened, a sinister undertone threading through the festive quiet. The hearth's light wavered, casting shadows that danced too freely, as if answering the locket's silent call. Outside, snow fell thicker, veiling the path, while the village's carols faded to a distant murmur, leaving Theo alone with the cottage's weight.

Theo's solitude, once a comfort, now pressed like the vines against the walls. Lydia's absence ached, a sad echo in the locket's gleam, yet her memory urged him forward, a faint romantic pull to their shared past. The note's warning lingered, its words a riddle he itched to solve. He scoffed again, softer, at the notion of spirits, yet the cottage's air grew heavy, the vines' scratch a chorus of subtle dread. His fingers trembled, hovering over the locket, its silver cool against his skin, promising answers to questions he dared not voice. The fire dimmed, as if the room held its breath, awaiting his choice.

As midnight bells tolled, their chime cutting through the frost, Theo opened the locket. Its cursed pulse, a spectral sigh, stirred the air, rousing frost kin from the festive dark, promising answers to unvoiced dread.

The locket's pulse flared, not from silver but hearthside shadows, shaping Miriam Caldwell's lace-clad shade, her eyes sharp as frozen holly thorns. Theodore Whitaker stumbled back, his spectacles fogging with quickened breath, the Bindweed Path cottage's dim hearth casting flickers across the parlor. The air thickened, heavy with a chill that belied the fire's glow, as Miriam's form wavered, her presence a violation of reason. "You've stirred me," she said, her voice a mournful melody laced with wry mirth, jarring Theo's ordered mind. The cottage, its stone walls snared by snow-draped vines, seemed to contract, the festive hush of Christmas Eve 2025 now a stage for unvoiced dread.

Theo gripped the locket, its holly etchings biting into his palm. "Who speaks?" he demanded, his voice steady despite the tremor in his chest. "Miriam Caldwell," she replied, her smile flickering, comical in its ghostly mismatch, like a jest played by the shadows. "Bound in 1852 by Edmund Hargrave, your kin, for a Yuletide betrayal." Her tale unfolded with measured cadence, each word heavy with sorrow. Hargrave, a scholar of forbidden studies, had sealed her spirit in the locket to hide his transgression, a vow broken under holly's boughs during a winter ritual. The curse siphoned warmth from its wielders, binding their souls to hers in an eternal debt. Theo's curiosity, once a scholar's spark, softened to empathy, her loss twinning Lydia's absence, five winters gone, a wound still raw in his heart.

He stepped closer, the hearth's light catching Miriam's lace, its delicate threads shimmering like frost on a frozen pane. "I've lost too," he confided, his voice hushed, the ache of Lydia's memory rising like a tide. Her laughter over garlands, her touch at midnight toasts, lingered in the cottage's quiet, a sad echo mirrored in Miriam's mournful gaze. Her touch, chill yet electric, brushed his hand, kindling a forbidden spark that wove romance through their shared sorrow. "We vowed under holly," she murmured, her words evoking Lydia's warmth, a fleeting promise of connection across the thinning veil. The locket clicked errantly mid-tale, a sharp snap that drew Theo's dry laugh. "Even shades miss their mark," he said, the humor a brief respite from the gathering dread.

The cottage's air grew colder, the vines outside writhing against frosted panes, their rustle a chilling chorus that mirrored bindweed's relentless climb. Miriam's story deepened, her voice threading visions into Theo's mind: Hargrave's ink-stained hands, a frostbound vow shattered under winter stars, his betrayal sealing her fate in silver. Shadows in the parlor sighed replies, faint wails of trapped souls, amplifying the supernatural tension. The hearth flickered, its glow faltering as if starved by the curse's hunger. Theo's logic clashed with empathy, his scholar's mind grappling with the locket's unnatural power. The cottage, once a haven, turned into a cage, its vine-choked walls reflecting his entanglement in Miriam's eternal plight.

Miriam's gaze softened, her vulnerability a lure, yet her words carried a sinister edge. "The locket binds us," she said, her voice low, almost pleading. "Its warmth is ours." The air tightened, the hearth's light dimming further, as vines outside rattled with unnatural vigor. Theo's heart quickened, Lydia's memory urging resistance, her echo a faint beacon in the growing dark. He clutched the locket, its pulse stronger now, each beat siphoning his warmth, a subtle drain that left his fingers numb. The grandfather clock's ticks grew erratic, marking time's unraveling as the solstice veil thinned further, a portal to the unseen.

He paced, the threadbare rug muffling his steps, but the vines' rustle drowned all else, a relentless reminder of the curse's hold. Miriam's form wavered, her lace catching the firelight, her eyes now hollowing with a possessive glint. "Stay," she urged, her voice a lover's plea laced with menace, her touch colder, more insistent. Theo's empathy faltered, fear rising as the cottage's walls seemed to pulse, the vines creeping inward, their tendrils piercing floorboards like holly thorns. Visions flashed again: Hargrave's betrayal, a ritual under snow-laden boughs, Miriam's scream trapped in silver, her eyes pleading for release. The locket's pulse quickened, its curse a tangible weight, binding Theo to its will.

He shook his head, clinging to logic, yet Miriam's allure tugged harder, her romantic pull darkening into a trap. Lydia's memory surged, her voice a whisper through the chaos, urging him to resist the locket's call. The hearth's embers sputtered, casting long shadows that danced with the vines' rhythm, a supernatural chorus echoing the locket's power. Theo's breath caught, his spectacles slipping as he studied Miriam's form, her beauty now a mask for the curse's hunger. The cottage groaned, its stones shifting under the vines' grip, a mirror to his own entanglement in this Yuletide haunt.

Theo's fingers tightened on the locket, its holly etchings sharp against his skin, a reminder of the note's warning: Holly curse stirs frost kin. His mind raced, piecing together Hargrave's folly, the scholar's arrogance that bound Miriam and others to this relic. The parlor's air grew stifling, the hearth's warmth all but gone, replaced by a chill that seeped into his bones. Miriam's gaze locked with his, her eyes now voids, her voice a hiss. "You cannot leave," she said, the words a command, her form swelling as shadows thickened around her. The vines' rustle became a roar, their tendrils snaking across the floor, curling toward Theo's feet, a bindweed snare tightening with each heartbeat.

He staggered back, the locket burning cold in his hand, its pulse a relentless drum. Lydia's echo grew louder, her warmth a faint guide through the dread, urging him to break free. The cottage's walls seemed to close in, the vines' chorus a chilling anthem of entrapment. Theo's empathy battled fear, his scholar's resolve fraying under Miriam's possessive stare. The locket clicked again, a mocking jest that spurred another dry laugh, a fleeting spark of humor in the darkening haunt. Yet the curse's grip tightened, its holly-bound dread a noose around his warmth, pulling him toward Miriam's eternal fate.

As Miriam's gaze turned ravenous, vines piercing floorboards like holly thorns, Theo grasped the locket curse, its dread ensnaring his warmth in winter's chilling weave.

Vines snared Theo's ankles like holly thorns, Miriam Caldwell's shade darkening as Hargrave's curse surged, her sigh twisting into a ravenous claim. The Bindweed Path cottage groaned, its stone walls pulsing under snow-draped vines, the parlor's hearth casting feeble flickers against the Christmas Eve dark of 2025. Theodore Whitaker's breath caught, his spectacles slipping as he clutched the silver locket, its holly etchings biting his palm. The air turned stifling, the curse's chill seeping into his bones, drowning festive warmth. Miriam's form swelled, her lace-clad figure looming, her eyes voids of hunger, no longer the mournful shade he pitied but a specter bent on claiming him wholly.

Visions flooded Theo's mind, vivid as the hearth's dying embers. Edmund Hargrave, his ancestor, in 1852, his ink-stained hands sealing Miriam's fate under snow-laden boughs. A forbidden ritual, a vow broken for arcane knowledge, trapped her scream in silver, forging the locket's curse in a Yuletide betrayal. Each image burned, a stab of dread revealing Hargrave's arrogance binding souls to an eternal debt. Lydia's echo flickered through the chaos, her voice a beacon from their shared Christmases, lost to five winters' grief. Her laughter over garlands, her gentle touch at midnight toasts, urged defiance, a call to break the curse's hold. Theo's heart pounded, his scholar's logic fraying under the locket's relentless pulse, each beat siphoning his warmth, numbing his fingers.

The cottage, once a haven, was a cage, its vine-choked walls alive with the curse's hunger. Vines rustled outside, their chilling chorus mirroring bindweed's grip, snaking closer through frosted panes, their tendrils coiling in the dim light. Miriam's voice hissed, "Stay with me," her words a lover's plea turned sinister, her chill touch a chain seeking to bind him forever. Theo's empathy, kindled by her tale of betrayal, battled rising fear, the locket's pulse a drum draining his warmth. Lydia's memory surged, her echo a sad anchor tying him to life, her voice whispering, "Break it," a plea to shatter the curse mirroring his solitude.

Theo's resolve hardened, his fear yielding to empathy's clarity: the locket's curse was his isolation's mirror, a trap he refused to abide. "No more chains," he vowed, his voice steady, wrenching his legs free from the vines' thorny grasp. He raised the locket, its silver gleaming in the hearth's faltering light, and smashed it against the stone mantel with desperate force. Silver shards erupted, a whirlwind of sighs bursting forth: Miriam's anguished cry, Lydia's gentle whisper, Hargrave's regretful moan, each voice a thread in the curse's unraveling. The room quaked, the vines' chorus faltering, a shard clicking defiantly on the floor, a jest amid chaos drawing

Theo's fleeting smile, a spark of humor in the supernatural storm.

Miriam's form softened, her eyes regaining mournful gleam, no longer ravenous but tender. "You've freed us," she breathed, her voice a sigh sealing a fleeting bond, her lace-clad hand brushing Theo's with a final spark of romance, echoing Lydia's warmth from winter's past. Her gaze lingered, a poignant farewell, tying their shared grief across centuries. The visions faded, Hargrave's regret lingering as a redeemed shadow, his ancestral folly undone by Theo's courageous act. Lydia's echo pulsed stronger, her presence guiding Theo toward life, her memory a bridge between Miriam's release and his salvation. The vines retreated, slinking back through floorboards, the cottage's walls exhaling as if freed from bindweed's choke, its stone no longer a prison but a protective shield.

The hearth flickered to life, its glow piercing frost coating the parlor's panes, warming the air with tentative promise. The grandfather clock resumed steady ticks, time reclaiming rhythm as the solstice veil thickened. Theo's solitude, long a heavy weight, lifted, his heart opening to the hope of renewal. The curse's grip dissolved, the locket's shards silent, their holly etchings dulled in firelight. Miriam's shade faded, her farewell sigh a poignant echo, tying Theo's grief to her release, a sad yet freeing farewell softening the night's lingering dread.

Outside, snow fell softer, the village's drone-lit carols a distant hum, their festive cheer no longer a mockery but an invitation to rejoin the world. Theo's fear vanished, replaced by empathy's triumph, his inner arc complete as he recognized his solitude's end. Hargrave's shadow rested, his regret redeemed through Theo's courage. The hearth's warmth spread, melting frost's grip, symbolizing life's return. Theo stepped toward the door, the locket's curse a fading memory, its dread no longer binding his heart. The parlor's air lightened, the vines' rustle stilled, the cottage a sanctuary reborn under dawn's quiet glow.

Dawn warmed the hearth through frost, Theo stepping into snow, bells tolling life's promise, his solitude fading beneath the holly locket curse.

17

Sarah Hozumi

The Second Tree

As was tradition, we went out in late afternoon with our grandmother to the woods behind her house, searching for the right pine tree to dig up, then decorate that evening.

Eira had one arm around our grandmother's waist to help steady her in the uneven snow as we trudged along. I balanced a shovel in one hand and a rope tied to a sled in the other, which bobbed along behind me like the happiest kid in the world.

The trail led us along the edge of a cemetery that was spreading out like a cloak over the years as it smothered the trees and wildlife with its bright white and gray headstones. The waist-high, black metal fence around its perimeter did little to deter deer from hopping over it and enjoying flowers laid in front of the graves, so every time I visited my grandmother, I'd see the groundskeeper patrolling the fence with a hunting rifle in hand early in the mornings.

I scanned among the headstones in case he was kneeling down to tend to some weeds and saw the massive pine tree near the center of the grounds, its brown needles and half the branches gone. The groundskeeper was usually fussing over the tree in the afternoons, but he wasn't there now, and by the looks of the decrepit tree, he hadn't been there for a while.

Eira and my grandmother were well ahead of me by that point, even with my grandmother hobbling along in the snow, and I realized I'd been standing there, staring at the dying pine tree for far too long. With a quick shiver racing up my chest as the cold wormed its way through my layers of clothing, I hugged the shovel and bounded after them.

"There," our grandmother said a few minutes later, pointing at a pine tree nearly as tall as I was.

"Lovely," Eira said. She helped our grandmother lean against a larger tree nearby before going with me to our prize. We used our gloved hands to push the snow aside until we reached the dirt surrounding the base of the trunk, then I took my shovel and got to work digging, stepping on its metal edge when the frozen ground forbade me from digging deeper.

Sweat dripped down my brow ten minutes into it, and I glared at my sister for not helping. Her back was turned to me, I realized, and she stood ramrod straight, like a wooden toy.

"Eira?"

My voice seemed to jolt her out of whatever daydream she was in, and with a quick shake of her head, she turned to me and blinked a few times before giving a weak smile.

"I could use some help."

"Yeah okay." Her voice was unusually quiet, low.

We worked in silence, any chance of horsing around abandoned as my sister kept looking to her left like someone was watching us. Of course, I kept looking, too, but there was nothing.

About a half hour later, fingers frozen solid, we managed to haul the tree out of the ground and heft it onto the sled. With Eira having to help my grandmother again, I was left to deal with the shovel and the tree. The entire operation was awkward, but it was only about a ten minutes' walk to our grandmother's house, then I could spend the rest of the day by the fire, drinking hot tea and complaining to anyone who'd listen about how hard it'd been.

***

We reached the edge of our grandmother's house, and I rested the tree against the siding before pulling the sled out from under it. Eira helped our grandmother inside while I went to the hose so I could clean the shovel off.

A few more minutes, and I'll be warm, I inwardly chanted as the frosty water splashed against my fingers. The dirt began to run off as mud while I heard my uncles and cousins coming outside, hauling the tree into a prepared pot, then dragging it into the house, where a roar of cheers greeted them. The edges of the pot always dug into my skin when I'd had to help lift previous years' trees into the house, which was why I'd practically begged for the chance to dig up the tree this year. Having actually done it, though, I was no longer sure which chore was worse.

My thoughts were on plastic trees and how they could solve all of our problems when I felt someone's ice-cold fingers touch the back of my neck.

I jumped and turned to destroy whoever thought it hilarious to sneak up on me like that, and I found Eira standing stock still in front of me, her arms bolted to her sides. There was a bright blue tint to her brown irises, her mouth slightly open.

"Eira?"

"Come with me." Her voice was low again, like she was half asleep.

"What? Why?"

"Bring the shovel. Bring the sled."

She started walking back into the forest, down the trail we'd just taken. The sun was starting to set, though, and our parents had always told us to never wander into the woods in the dark. Seeing Eira disappear into shadows, every story they'd told us came crawling back into the forefront of my thoughts: Mostly stories of ghosts eating children who wandered alone at night.

"Eira!"

With a fantastic swear under my breath, I grabbed the frozen shovel and the dirt-covered sled and chased after her. I called her name again as I ran along the trail, the sled whipping the trees behind me, and I nearly ran right past her.

She was off to the left, her hand hovering in front of a tree that barely reached her waist.

"This one." Her voice was a whisper, and in the stillness of the woods, the unnatural tone went right through me like a blast of frozen air.

"Why?"

And Eira's horribly bright blue eyes were on me, practically glowing in the long shadows the sun cast as it breathed its last for the day.

"They are waiting."

Her glowing eyes were locked on mine, her face relaxed into a blank stare I only saw her make just before falling asleep. One of her hands still hovered right above the tree, but the rest of her had fallen into place like a statue. My lone comfort was I could still hear her breathing.

What was going on?

"You want me to dig this tree up? Why?"

"They are waiting."

"Listen, just stay here, I'll go get help." I let go of the sled's rope and clutched the shovel to my chest like a talisman. "Don't move."

Just as I was about to turn and make a run for it to the house, to scream for help from anyone who could hear, I saw three blue lights glaring from the cemetery. Little flames floating in the winter air, brighter than even the last bursts of sunlight for the day.

"Hey, do you see those lights?"

"They are waiting," Eira said for a third time.

Thoughts of running for help dissipated, and I turned to face my sister again.

"All right, I'll help you, but then you have to let my sister go."

What am I saying, I thought. I couldn't honestly be thinking something was possessing my sister. I immediately blamed my parents for telling us too many horror stories about the woods when we were growing up.

"Of course." Why was she playing into the lunacy?

Nothing making sense whatsoever, my brain at least could piece together the conclusion that it was getting dark out. Though the tree she'd chosen probably wouldn't take as long to dig out of the ground, I was still exhausted from the first tree, and the ground was only getting colder now that the sun wasn't even attempting to warm it anymore.

Would anyone come looking for us?

I got to work clearing the snow away like I had for the first tree. It was slow, painful work, and the sun had long since set by the time I finally felt the tree loosen enough that I could begin pulling at it. Eira came over and helped, at least. An owl cried out in the distance just as we pulled the tree out of the ground. A twisted, entirely unbecoming smile enveloped Eira's mouth as she helped me carry it to the sled, then she immediately set out again.

I barely had time to grab the sled, steadying the tree with my free hand, before she'd disappeared into the thick shadows. At least I knew where she was going, though – the lights were still there, watching us.

Watching us?

I pulled the sled along, feeling both alone and like I was being followed, until I nearly crashed into Eira. She stood against the black fence of the cemetery, her hand pointing to a clearing among the headstones.

"There."

What had been three lights were now ten, possibly more.

Exhaustion and pure terror had ground down my need to understand what was happening, and so instead of demanding answers I knew she would never give, I simply nodded once.

Eira helped me hoist the tree over the fence, her arms returning to their sides as the tree slid off one of the headstones before crashing to the ground with a rustling thud. My arms felt more like liquid than muscle by that point, but I managed to heft myself over the fence as well. I stood between two smaller headstones and turned to help Eira over.

It was like she'd forgotten how to use her arms and legs. Everything was wearing down on my patience, but none so much as the insistent, blank look to her even as her leg caught on the fence. Some part of me understood I had to get this done, though. If I wanted my sister back again, I had to get this thing done. And so, I helped guide her one step at a time until she was finally over.

"Thank you."

Same blank stare, same dreamlike voice. Instead of bothering to reply, I grunted at her and grabbed the tree by its trunk, dragging it through the snow.

A sea of blue flames greeted us. It felt in a lot of ways like looking at a galaxy at a planetarium, with each fire a star that began to orbit me as soon as I came closer with the tree in hand.

There was already a hole in the ground, a mound of dirt nearby, and no part of me stopped to wonder why there might be in a cemetery as I moved the tree until it was standing. Eira held the top for me, at least, while I pushed the mound of freshly dug-up earth around it, then stamped my foot around the base.

For a solid moment, I simply stood there, gasping for air, sweat stinging my eyes, admiring what I had accomplished. I'd managed to dig up two trees in one winter's day. That was something to be proud of.

"Thank you."

I nearly jumped to hear Eira's voice right beside me, and I saw the blue was still there, now glowing in the night.

"You said I could have her back again." I still didn't even know what that meant. Was I really going to play along with all of this?

"Wait." She gestured at the tree, her arm still stiff like a doll's.

The fires were hovering closer and closer to the tree, ebbing and flowing like waves against the shore, until they began to attach themselves to the branches. The tree, in return, seemed to spring to life, swaying in the wind as the lights glittered against its needles. It soon became so covered that it began to look like a firework in the outline of a tree.

And then, the wind stopped, and I took a step behind Eira. Even though a great part of me understood she wasn't my sister anymore, I still found myself reaching for her hand when I saw the faint outlines of people wandering toward the tree. Her frozen fingers curled around mine, and I found slight comfort as the people gathered around it.

"You have done a great thing for us," Eira said as the people began to sway back and forth. "Our old tree will die soon, and we needed a new one."

"And...I can have my sister back?"

"As promised. I will walk with you to the edge, and you must promise me to not look upon us again once you cross to the other side."

Her grip on my hand tightened as she led me back to the black fencing surrounding the cemetery. I looked back at the people as they began to walk in circles around the tree, holding hands. Some of them seemed so small, no bigger than my youngest cousin.

"We will call upon you again next year if needed."

A stab of fear punctured my lungs, but I still managed to throw myself over the fence while looking outward. I then heard Eira fighting her away across, too. I wanted to turn and help, but I couldn't look. Instinct drove me to keep my eyesight forward. And so, I waited.

She landed with a heavy thud beside me, gasping so loudly that I nearly did look back at her.

"What are we still doing outside?" Out of the corner of my eye, I saw her looking around. I grabbed her hand and started to pull her toward the house. "Ow, that's too tight. What's going on?"

"Nothing, nothing, but we have to go home."

"What? Why? Where are we?"

She was going to turn around. I couldn't have her turn around.

"The shovel is just up ahead. I left it out by accident. You said you'd help me go get it, remember?"

I had to get Eira out of there.

"But we dug up a tree more back that way, right?"

I could feel her arm tugging against mine as she was probably trying to turn around. She would see the people in the cemetery, and I'd lose her forever.

"No!"

Eira wrenched her hand out of mine, but I still couldn't look back to face her. I could only pray.

"Why are we really out here?"

"Because…" I closed my eyes and turned to face her, "because something happened–"

"Matthew, look!"

It took all of my willpower not to open my eyes. She grabbed my shoulders and forced me to turn, though, away from the cemetery. I opened my eyelids by a fraction of a degree before they flew open in pure wonder.

Two deer stood before us, gazing at us with magnificent indifference. We stared at them in reverence; they tolerated us for a fraction of a second longer before sauntering away into the depths of the woods.

***

Our parents ordered us to sit in front of the fireplace once we'd returned. For a second, the living room was quiet as everyone got to work reheating our dinner, my uncle calling from the kitchen window to my cousins who had gone out to look for us. Eira was beside me, gazing into the fire.

"See anything interesting?"

Our grandmother intently gazed at us from her rocking chair across the coffee table.

"Nothing I really want to remember," I muttered.

"When I was about your age, Matthew, I remember helping my friend Gabriel dig up a tree as the sun set on a night like this one. He had this look to his eyes that made me think he was possessed by a ghost."

Both Eira and I shuddered nearly at the same time.

"Well, after we dug up a tree, he had me drag it all the way into the cemetery, which was a lot smaller then. There was a hole already there, waiting for us, and he told me to put the tree into that hole. It was the first time I'd ever dug up a tree instead of chopping it down. I planted it there with his help, and then the tree lit up all on its own. Gabriel loved it so much, he loved that tree so much, he started working there, you know, at the cemetery, to protect the tree. He said it lit up every year, but I only saw the one. His son works there now. Did I tell you that?"

"No." My voice diminished in fear as I remembered whatever had taken hold of Eira saying something about never leaving. "He likes it there?"

"As far as I know. It can be hard work protecting a tree like that. And I think, like many traditions, there are times when you don't feel like doing them anymore. Traditions have a way of getting done all the same." And she winked at both of us. "Maybe you two have found a new tradition, too?"

"Maybe," I said, and Eira's gaze fell to the carpet while I took to staring at my hands. "Does it have to be?"

"I honestly don't know. Gabriel sometimes said he had no choice, and I'm sure his son might have no say in the matter, either, but at least you're making people happy. Surely that has to count for something."

"A tradition worth doing." The words twisted and curled out of my mouth in odd tones and pitches, like someone was saying them for me, but I felt a kind of warmth to them that teased me into feelings of contentment. "I think I did find something worth doing."

"Good." There was the tiniest hint of blue to her gray eyes as she smiled at me, and I found myself smiling back, the joy of helping out enveloping any need for fear. "I'm so glad, Matthew."

18

Amber Willis

Grab the Christmas Cookies

The windshield wipers swiped once, clearing the few snowflakes hugging the window. The neighbor's reindeer display was scattered, eight mangled plastic hunks thrown from Santa's sleigh, shattered glass covered Donner. I placed a clammy hand to my throbbing forehead, the decorations blinked merrily in the drifting snow, calm and bright. I glanced at my sister in the passenger seat; Bethany smiled. "Thanks for picking me up, again. I'm sorry you always have to drive me everywhere. One day I'll get a decent car, and you won't have to worry about toting me around everywhere."

"Oh honey, no worries! I don't mind at all. I enjoy the company. Anytime. I'm just glad to have you along." I cranked up the radio and began singing along to "Deck the Halls," pretending I didn't see the neighbor's décor; no, never happened.

"I hope Aunt Clara makes her homemade yeast rolls again. Those are my favorite. I've dreamed about those all year." Bethany flipped the vent upward, turning the heat from blowing her round face.

"I'm sure she will. She always does." I reluctantly turned the heat down a notch, not wanting to roast my sister. Well, maybe I did a little, but I wanted her to be comfortable.

I turned on my left turn signal at the stop sign. A white, two-story house flashed with piercing, red strobe lights. Swirling, menacing flashes of an ambulance. My heart ached for the people inside; the trauma being endured on what is supposed to be a festive occasion. I shut my eyes, trying to force my tear ducts closed. I looked back at the house as "Fa la la la la" thumped through my speakers. Tiny crimson lights happily chased themselves around the porch and around the edges of the house, contently flashing in harmony. Everything was serene in the fresh snow.

"I love seeing everyone's Christmas decorations." Bethany stared out her window.

"Yeah, it is nice to see while you're out travelling around. Don't see any spiders anywhere, though."

"Spiders? That's Halloween, goofy."

"Well, in some countries, spiders are seen as good luck and are used in Christmas décor."

"Well, in this country, you are a nerd, and nobody cares about your weird Christmas facts."

"Well, missy, in this car, I am the queen of nerds and my weird facts reign. For instance, did you know it used to be illegal to celebrate Christmas? It was seen as too pagan and was unacceptable for Christians to participate in."

"Ugh!"

Gravel and glittering snow crunched under my tires as we pulled into Aunt Clara's driveway. Her house was covered in blue icicle lights and blow mold snowman covered the yard like a frosty army paroling the winter wonderland. I parked next to my uncle's rusted pickup. "Can you carry those gingerbread cookies for me?" I nodded to the round, plastic tub.

"Oooo, I like to bite the little heads off the gingerbread men." Bethany grinned.

"Well, you'll have to settle for beheading dinosaurs." I giggled.

"Dinosaurs?! You nerd! That's not Christmasy. Leave it to you."

"It could be worse. I found a cookie cutter of a frog dissection. Coulda went with that; nice red icing for the heart, brown for the intestines."

"Science nerd." Bethany rolled her icy blue eyes.

"Just grab the cookies, will ya?"

"Uhm, hey Kim. You need help? I can grab the cookies for you." My cousin Laura smiled, her compassionate brown eyes full of concern.

I looked at the empty passenger seat, tears easing over my pale cheeks. "Yeah, okay, thanks, Laura." I muttered, my lips quivered as I tried to compose myself.

"You're welcome. Are you doing okay? I know this must be hard on you; it is on all of us. We all miss her. Hard to believe it's been a year." Laura tucked my gingerbread dinos under one arm and hugged me with the other.

"It's fine. I'm fine." I turned from her and hurried to my aunt's door.

"Hey Kim!" I heard various voices call, my aunt maybe. I don't know. I hurried to the bathroom and slammed the door behind me. I pressed my back to the door and slid to the floor; my hands tangled in my hair and pulled.

***

"I thought you got a car. Didn't you just get a used car? What's wrong with that?" I grumbled.

"I did, but it's really used. The headlights are awful, and I can't see well in it. It isn't the most reliable thing and needs more work. I'm just afraid to drive it right now. Please, Kim." Bethany asked.

"Seriously? I'm not always going to be around to give you a free ride. If you want to go to the dinner, drive yourself! I'm not your babysitter, Bethany."

"Okay, Kim. I'm sorry. I'll drive. It's not snowing now, I'll go slow. I'm sorry I bothered you."

"Good. See you at Aunt Clara's." I jabbed the red button on my cell. Times like this I wish I had a landline so I could slam the phone down. Jabbing a button just wasn't the same.

I showered and pulled on my new tacky Christmas sweater, complete with battery powered Christmas lights and tinsel. I grabbed my box of homemade cookies and hopped into my car. I turned to the left at the stop sign and proceeded toward my aunt's Christmas party. Up ahead, a woman burst out of her front door and ran down her porch, her hand flew to her gapping mouth. I slowed and watched her as she began to scream. I turned my head to follow her gaze. Eight battered reindeer were strewn across the lawn. Donner glittered with broken glass. Splashes of crimson slithered around the deer like Santa's reins. A rusty, very used car was smashed tightly into Santa's warped sleigh. A body, oh God, ran rivers of holly red, neatly blending with the holiday cheery colors. A body, her body, grew cold in the Christmas air. Piercing red lights strobed across her crumpled form as sirens pulsated in my throbbing ears. They covered Bethany with a white sheet and loaded her into the ambulance.

***

I pulled at my curls. She just wanted a ride; I could have given her that.

19

Callum J. McCready

Christmas Mourning

Christmas was the day they met.
Christmas was the day she died.
Christmas was the day she came back…

Red water ran for Michael Francis.
    The family were concerned for his well-being. Despite entreaties to the contrary, he turned at the notion of visitors during the holidays this year. What his remaining adult children or those grandchildren who still spoke to him didn't know was that Michael Francis was never truly alone…

- 2025 -

He woke late on Christmas morning. He'd been doing that a lot. Some days he didn't even bother to get out of bed, lest he run the risk of falling over again, have to ring for someone to come pick him up off the floor. Unsteady on his feet, though he'd never admit as much, he ignored medical advice and was now nearly blind and deaf as a post. He hadn't eaten a proper meal in thirteen days. Advanced years and a rapid decline, sitting long well into the night drinking Smirnoff and Diet Cokes mixed half-and-half, eating sweets by the dozen in defiance of diabetes in the recliner chair by the apartment window overlooking the graveyard below made the prospect of his days grim, if not null and void. Not that he had much to look forward to, anyway, except death, maybe. "Least I don't have far to go," he'd chime in to himself or no one. Getting old was a miserable business, and Michael Francis felt every bit of it, too tired to even be angry any more.

Troubled as much by internal musings as a perpetual hangover, he got out of his chair, slowly shuffling as he felt his way across the carpet on to the tiled floor of the kitchenette to take a small glass from the cupboard just above on his right. Holding it under the tap in the sink, he turned the handle. Despite failing sight, he couldn't help noticing that red water ran from the tap. He could have dismissed it as a dirty pipe, but that was when he knew she'd come back.

Then again, she'd never really left.

"Rouge..."

- 1958 -

Mickey Francis immigrated from West Belfast to America, passing through Ellis Island like countless others before him and many more after, working in a factory on weekdays and boxing at weekends before receiving his draft notice.

Mickey and two of his fellow soldiers were on leave from Bayern-Kaserne in Munich partying up a storm across the western city of San Francisco when they wound up in a pub frequented by working ladies. Although partial to a bit on the side, Mickey had a rule about paying for sex, believing it to be beneath him not to be able to get a woman into bed through charm alone. That all changed when he saw her.

Rouge.

Although it wasn't unheard of for a woman of darker complexion to be found in southern dive bars or to take up sex work as a chosen trade and profession, it was unusual to meet one carrying herself with such ease, grace and confidence. If he ever read a book instead of scowling at them the word he might have used would be 'ethereal' to describe her. There was an earthy quality mingled with otherworldliness, a supernatural aspect making her stand out. While not unconscious of her place in a country with historical issues surrounding race, she was not only an exceptionally attractive young woman but possessed a soul which radiated from her pores in a black floral dress patterned with large red roses, one probably a tad more expensive than the usual moll frippery. Mickey didn't have much time for clothes but he scrubbed up well.

Approaching while she sat with her friends, he felt draw by a magnetic force akin to hypnosis, an aura indicating essence, purity. Introducing himself, she slowly stood up as he took her hand, stealing a kiss on the back of it as she smiled in return, uttering a single syllable from red-matte lips, "Rouge," a sound which, despite the noise and relatively rowdy bar, rang out like the sonorous sooth-song of music to his then-functional ears.

After a few more drinks and dancing, Mickey dragged her, his buddies and their women to another place which, on paper, was supposed to be more upmarket but came across as bush-league in attempting to be something it wasn't. Crossing the threshold of hanging mistletoe and tinsel, Mickey ordered six pints, counting out a handful of bills as the barkeep placed down five.

Noticing the absent drink, Mickey pointed out, "I ordered six, pal."

Staring straight into the deep void of dead space, refusing to make eye contact with anyone, the southern man drawled out like a monotone third-rate Jackie Gleason, "We don't serve their kind here."

A moment or two followed not dissimilar to that of two gunfighters standing six paces apart, as though each was waiting to see who'd make the first move. The barkeep didn't have to wait. Mickey, while generally passing well and hospitably accommodated by his adopted country, had encountered anti-Irish sentiment at home and abroad and had an even lower tolerance for bullshit.

"Take your pints and stick 'em up your arse!" Catching Rouge in his arms, he swung her round, leaning in to kiss her under the mistletoe. Although already sold on her, it was that moment which sold her on him, and whether it was a certain, innate crazy streak in both as anything involving actual romance, Mickey and Rouge became something of an item.

***

Born of a light-skinned French-Algiers mother and an African-American father, she grew up in a mixed-race household which, in the days of miscegenation, would have been considered unusual, to some even taboo, but times were changing. The years would bear fruit to progress. Like him, she was twenty years old, and any time he got off he'd be straight on over to spend as many hours as he could with her.

Laying naked on the beds of cheap boarding-houses across the state over from one another, in between fitful bouts of lovemaking they'd drift in and out of sleep, but more often as not talk the night away, about their pasts, about their lives, about their future, anything and everything in between. Regardless of the differences in their respective backgrounds and make-up, they considered these details marginal at best, and in many regards their hopes and dreams matched up. Despite relative youth, both had been around the horn a bit and for the first time had met someone with whom they had synergy, had developed a legitimate connection.

Sometimes Rouge would embarrass him by bringing out one of the letters he had written her from his station, and she'd laugh as he blushed, pretending to snarl, but really it warmed his heart. Despite playing hard at trying to be a tough guy, he was a closeted romantic at heart. Rouge's endearing kindnesses, understanding and empathy brought out a softness and gentle quality that Mickey didn't know he had in him.

At times, on more drunken nights, the wild sprees which occasionally saw them stumbling from tavern to tavern, later to the few opium dens still existing underground, they smoked themselves into oblivion, a black tar pit at the bottom of which only they and they existed, mad, delirious, and it was then that they'd made their pledges, blood rituals, insane declarations of everlasting love and life eternal. Although under the influence, they meant every bit of it, remembering everything.

She remembered everything. He did too, that is until

- *1959* -

he met Josie; a pretty, though quiet and unassuming young woman from the West of Mayo, fresh from a year in London employed as a shorthand writer, she'd got to New York on the boat from Liverpool to Ellis Island.

When honourably discharged he returned to the Bronx, continuing to box while sidling into a respectable job as an advertising salesman. Although sport was his passion, he was born with wit, looks and gift of the gab, the perfect fit for a social climber, man-about-town or, as one of his children would later declare, "a corner-boy," so eventually he went where the money talked.

Rouge would see him less and less but still received regular letters, written with the same simple but nevertheless affectionate words of faith and devotion. Rouge believed in

Mickey, continued to believe in him, more so than he would ever believe in himself.

Correspondence became less consistent, received more infrequently until, eventually, after trickling off to a dwindling drop, it stopped altogether. She was concerned, caring more for him than herself despite knowing, somewhere, at the back of her head, in her heart of hearts, that all was not well.

Then, one day, out of the blue, he came back. It was Christmas Eve, and after months of telling herself she was ready to move on, everything dissipated when she saw the crooked grin on his smiling face. Embracing, she noticed he'd put on a little weight, dressed in flashier cuts, cultivated that comfortable look people do when finances are no longer something to worry about.

When the moment came he sat her down and she understood that things had changed irrevocably, irreconcilably. He had looked up to her, and now, as he explained his dilemma, she realised it was now in fact she who needed him, but he didn't want her. Or at least he said he didn't. Perhaps it was to make it easier to extricate himself from a complicated situation, but as he bid her goodbye, she reminded him of the things they said, the days and nights they'd shared, how they would never leave or abandon one another. It was a marriage binding in all but the eyes of the law, built upon promises, extremity of emotion and the power of love. She would have given him the world, had let him know her, see her for who she was, but he turned away.

He broke their bond, and in that severance, Rouge too was broken beyond repair. The next night her body was found by a wino in a bottom-dwelling den, the coroner reporting death by deliberate overdose. Mickey found out a number of months down the line through the individual who'd served as his best man. He did what he felt any sensible man would do in the circumstances: go out on the town and get hammered.

***

Mickey and Josie eloped the month before Rouge's passing. Having met less than six months prior at a local dance largely populated by Irish immigrants North and South of the border, they embarked on an affair that saw Josie become pregnant. So as to avoid the ire of their staunchly Catholic families, the shame of a child born out of wedlock, they married before the end of the year and that of her term, moving into a small, three-room apartment in Queens.

Rouge's blood, that of a young woman, nameless, faceless, no one, was the taint, the sacrifice born of this union, and as they entered the sixties Mickey and Josie became parents to a baby girl. A second followed a year-and-a-half later, another when they re-settled in Ireland permanently. Mickey's much-wanted son came ten years later, sealing their fate for the decades that followed.

Taking over his father's business, he worked and worked and worked. His children married and they too had their own children. He devoted himself to his job, if not his wife. It was a loveless marriage, ("don't let him go," Mickey's mother said to her. "He'll never come back…"), the depression of which affected Josie and marked the upbringing of their progeny. He continued in this way until his early-eighties when his son took over the business from him.

There was a time when he had life about him, was the big man back home. Though he didn't exactly live a courageous life, was oftentimes difficult, occasionally cruel and abusive, there was an incredible force of personality, but the years beat him down and eventually defeated him.

- 2025 -

Sitting in his recliner chair by the window overlooking the graveyard, Michael supped the lazy cocktail, no longer receiving pleasure from consumption, only doing so out of habit, snarling bitterly once more, "Least I don't have far to go…"

His intake increased exponentially in the wake of the long-suffering Josie's passing, flaring up his outstanding health issues, even more so after Elsa, his eldest daughter and primary carer. He never appreciated his wife. Now, however much a nuisance and a burden he proclaimed her to be when alive, he found that he missed her. The rest of them were trying to put him in a home. They said it was for the best. He said he knew better, however desperate he really knew his situation to be.

The years, all those years, moments lost to time and eternity... His friends were dead, as were his siblings, "The Fighting Frankies," as his brother-in-law used to refer to them. He too was dead, and all he had left were thoughts and memories, restlessness, nightmares and ultimately, guilt and regret at what could have been, but there was a part of him that knew *she* had never really left him. He drank to dull the senses but felt her presence permeate from the walls, the vibrations of the interior space he inhabited.

"Come on... I know you're there. Show yourself..."

He felt something, or someone, take the glass of red liquid from his hand, the light brush of those warm, unmistakable fingers, membranes as familiar as his own, raising the hairs upon his forearm as Rouge walked around the side of his chair. Despite cataract-riddled vision in the gloomy grey overcast of an Irish winter's morning, he saw her clearly, standing there in her red-rose patterned black dress. "You came back..."

Turning her shoulder cooly towards him but not dispassionately, she spoke words which arrived to his weakened ears clear as day, "Yes, the same way you did," supping from the glass of red liquid before continuing. "The difference being *I* remembered. You didn't."

"That's not true... I remember *everything*. I tried to forget, but I couldn't. Do you know how it feels to carry that with you, every single day?"

"Yes," she supped, looking down at the graveyard outside the window as she leant against the rail. "I've wandered the earth more than half a century, carried it with me everywhere I went, a shade among the whole. What we did and said wasn't without meaning. It had purpose and intent, prevented me from attaining what I wanted, what I needed. Remember the things you said?" She turned towards him, echoing words from a time gone by: "'We may not be able to do the things we should, say the things we want to.' 'You are a prism, a beacon through which the ray of life's light shines out into the world.' 'You have inspired me, made me believe...' 'All these coincidences which, however meaningless or seemingly insignificant, amount to something altogether greater than their individual parts—'"

"Stop..."

"Oh, Michael... you were always at your best when you were at your most florid, a positive snake-charmer... 'Consider me your loyal and humble servant. I bow down and worship at thy feet, kiss the earth that they touch.' 'You have a force, an energy which glows, but it's your spirit which radiates most.' 'You are special, deserve nothing less than the utmost happiness.' 'As above, so below...'"

"Stop," he said again.

"'—Let me know your magic—'"

"STOP!" he roared with a force he didn't know was still in him. "Stop it now."

She smiled back the way she used to, but it now carried an indelible impression, that of knowledge and experience.

"Can't you see what I am? I'm beat, babe... broken, battered. I'm a husk, a shell of what I once was, a sad sack of shit, worn and withered down. I was never better than when I was with you. Every day since I've been eaten away, slowly first but now it's quicker, going faster than you can imagine. Do you know how it feels to *live* like this? It's a living death. Dogs have it better. I just wish they'd put me out of my misery..."

"Honey, you had a good life. You should try being alive *and* dead at the same time. Limbo's no picnic. Be grateful and stop feeling sorry for yourself."

"All that's left is pain. What do you want?"

"Absolution, and in return I can give you deliverance. All the time I knew you, Mick, you were fascinated by death. You grew up with it around you, had this drive, this compulsion to fight that was like an obsession which fascinated but also frightened you. That's why you never followed through with our pact. I'm here to help, show you things aren't all that bad."

"I thought you said you didn't like it."

"I don't like having my foot in both camps, if that's what you mean, but I've caught a glimpse of the other side. It's beautiful, really... Come on. Let's go. It's time."

"But I'm scared," he leant forward as she caught him in her arms. "I'm scared, Rouge... I'm scared of death, scared of life, everything..."

"Ssh," she whispered. "Momma's here. There's nothing to be afraid of. Remember: 'Hush-a-bye, don't you cry, Go to sleepy, little baby. Go to sleepy, little baby. When you wake, you shall have, all the pretty little horses.'"

It was then that it all came back to Michael Francis, only the tears he shed ran red, a water the colour of blood running down his cheeks, a weeping of sorrows which shed shackles, the bonds of life, forming a river into which he fell and flowed with Rouge, swimming off into the endless sea and joining her in death.

20

Nathan McKee

The Gift

It was the first time I had lied to my daughter, and it broke my heart. Her mum had dropped her off at 11, and I took her things up to her bedroom and left her there to settle in. When Elise came back downstairs, I was considering if the discounted loaf I picked up 3 days ago would still be ok if I just removed the moldy crusts. When she looked at the knife in my hand and asked what we were having for lunch, I lost my nerve.

"We're going to a restaurant, sweetheart, get your coat."

I would eat at the soup kitchen occasionally, but I swore I'd never bring Elise to one. I've always had good instincts as a father, the one area of my life where that's true. The thought of bringing her to a place filled with drug addicts, the mentally ill, and alcoholics was beyond the pale. Truth is, most of the people there were just like me: on the verge of poverty, trying to keep their head above water, struggling to float.

And to be fair to this place, it felt like a restaurant. Hope Ministries, they'd just opened recently, and were providing Christmas dinners in the lead up to the big day. We were greeted by a young girl, maybe 19 at most. She was pretty, but her short, black hair made her look boyish and her body hadn't filled out yet. Her name was Shannon according to the immaculate handwriting on her white nametag, she'd even drawn a smiley face in the "o" with the felt-tip pen.

Shannon haunched down and spoke directly to Elise before taking us to a table for two. She walked with the confidence of a rich, pretty university student volunteering in a soup kitchen for the homeless at Christmas, knowing she'd never have to be on the receiving end of such pity. I don't think she even looked at me once.

The table was set with a red tablecloth and real cutlery, normally these sorts of places make us use the bamboo knives that couldn't slice through butter without snapping in half. There was a glass each, a bottle of sparkling fruit juice, and a little jar of cranberry sauce. The smell of turkey, ham, and stuffing in the air was almost enough to mask the stench of long soiled clothing and the bodies that inhabited them.

I was fidgeting with a hole that had appeared in the cuff of my grey hoodie when another woman appeared beside us. Despite her grey hair and sagging cheeks, she had the air of a bird of prey. Her eyes seemed to fix on a point and her head would pivot to avoid losing track of her target. There was something unsettling about her presence and I thought she was another patron at first. Her name tag was decidedly less friendly than Shannon's: jagged black lines from a ballpoint pen scratched her name like runes on a cave wall, or something equally ancient.

"What'll you be having?" she said.

Nancy had something wrong with her mouth, maybe a tooth infection. When she spoke, eating was the last thing I could think of. I had once worked in an abattoir and I was worried the smell would stick to my clothes in the same way.

"Turkey and ham," I said, "For both of us."

"You sure?"

Nancy looked at Elise who looked at me before nodding. Elise wasn't a big meat eater but she rarely finished her plate, anyway. I thought if I was lucky, she'd leave me her wee cocktail sausages. She noted down our orders and turned away before remembering something.

"You didn't get one of the hampers on your way in, did you?"

"I didn't see any, they must all be gone."

"Oh, nonsense!" she said, with too much breath for my liking. "I'll make sure to bring one over, with a special gift just for you!"

Nancy pinched Elise's cheek and I nearly lunged for her. The unease I had felt since she first approached the table had opened into a deep pit within my stomach. My eyes darted to my daughters, wide and shining. I could tell my cheeks were burning red as the thoughts raced through my head: No, we couldn't possibly accept. We don't need charity, it's not right to accept handouts. This woman thought I couldn't provide for my own child, that I couldn't even get her a Christmas present. I thought about the doll I'd picked up at the charity shop, and the newspaper I'd wrapped it in.

"Can we, daddy? Can I have it?"

My body was screaming no.

"Sure, of course, sweetheart. That's very kind, thank you."

Nancy nodded with a smile that I found both genuine and smug. She returned a little while later with the hamper and left it on the floor beside our table. I didn't want to look desperate but I was curious what was in it. At a quick glance, I could make out some deodorant, tins of soup, and a scarf. Definitely one of the "single male" hampers. Behind the scarf, I could just about make out some wrapping paper, the present for Elise. I was expecting a selection box, but this was something much smaller. I wanted to take it, shake it, try to figure out what was inside. Maybe just tear the corner slightly and peek. I was about to reach for it when Shannon came by the table.

"I'm so sorry guys, it's really busy today. What'll you be having?"

I told her Nancy had already taken our order and she seemed confused. She checked with the kitchen and came back a moment later. She apologised again, she didn't know a Nancy and she mustn't have brought their order to the chefs, but soon enough we had our food.

It was me that didn't finish my plate, my appetite had gone. I played with my mashed potatoes while Elise told me about the nativity she'd played in - she was one of the wise men, I think. I'd been invited but in the way that it was clear I was supposed to say no. I tried to follow her story about how Joseph had stepped on one of the sheep's tails, but I was scanning the room, looking for any sign of Nancy. She seemed to have vanished.

***

We spent the afternoon in town together and I managed to forget about the strangeness at Hope Ministries. We'd had a light dusting of snow that hadn't completely turned to mush yet, and managed to build a mini snowman in the park.

It was already dark by the time we got home, and I told Elise to get into her reindeer pyjamas, bring her duvet downstairs, and we could watch whatever she wanted. I told her it'd give us more time together, but I was just hoping she'd fall asleep on the sofa, and I wouldn't have to turn on the heating in her room.

I was going through the hamper, looking for some snacks for us, when I remembered the present for Elise. The wrapping paper was old, maybe from the 70s. The present itself was a little bigger than a ring box, but it had quite a heft to it. Under the paper, I could feel carvings on the box. I thought they could be letters at first, but I couldn't make out anything legible. The unease came back as I held the gift, and I thought for a moment I could smell that same stench that had come from Nancy when she spoke. I had a strong desire to throw it in the bin and tell Elise we must have lost it in the park, but I'd already lowered myself by taking it in the first place, so it went under the tree. Elise came downstairs a short while later, I opened a beer, and we channel-hopped for a bit before finding a movie to watch.

The countdown to the 10 o'clock news reminded me that I'd fallen asleep. I looked from the screen to Elise and could tell from her breathing that she was not so deeply asleep that I could risk more than the slightest movement. I reached for the remote on the coffee table and switched off the TV. The sudden silence caused my ears to ring as I shut my eyes and drifted back into the warmth and numbness of sleep. When the high-pitched whine receded, I could hear something else beneath it. A familiar sound, the neighbours TV through the wall, I thought. It was comforting at first, and then curious. Since I had moved to the estate, Dave and Rachel had spent every Christmas at her parents' house. I held my breath and listened closer as one sense of familiarity was replaced by another.

Elise had been three at the time, and I was already sleeping on the sofa. I woke somewhere around 2 AM to the rhythmic tss-tss-tss of scratching behind the kitchen door. It would start and stop and I couldn't understand what I was hearing at first, but cold spread through my veins as the dread of certainty enveloped me. Someone had left the back door open late into the evening, and a rat had gotten in. I lay there for half an hour listening to the intermittent scratching when it suddenly stopped. I didn't sleep that night, wondering if it had somehow gotten into the rest of the house, or even made its way back outside. I called in sick to work – I was still working at that time – and when Elise came downstairs, I told her we had a surprise in the kitchen so her mum would take her out for breakfast before pre-school.

Once they had left, I braved the kitchen for the first time, but by the smell I could tell there was no more risk. I pulled out the washing machine, checked every cupboard and eventually found it. The rat had gone behind the fridge and sunk its teeth into the power cable. The heat back there must have sped things along, the stench clung to the walls until long after the divorce.

The sound was coming from the direction of the Christmas tree. I opened my eyes as wide as I could, but they were still adjusting to the darkness. It seemed for just a moment that the gift was moving. I shifted slightly to get a better look when, suddenly, there was silence. Maybe it was the relief, or the third beer, or something else, but I found myself drifting to sleep, powerless to investigate any further.

***

I woke up early the next morning, my head tender and my bladder screaming for relief. Elise wasn't on the sofa, but she'd left her duvet. I got up and went to the tree, hoping to see no sign of rats or mice, and then froze. Wrapping paper covered the floor, torn to shreds, and that little box was nowhere to be seen.

I was furious. In that moment, I could've throttled Elise. I had embarrassed myself, lowered myself by accepting that gift, and the little shit couldn't even wait until Christmas morning to open it. I flew up the stairs like a bullet and slammed into her bedroom door. It wouldn't budge but there was no lock. I screamed at her to open the door, but there was no response. After throwing my shoulder into it three or four more times, it suddenly gave way, the frame splintering, cutting my face. As the door swung into the room there was a whooshing sound like air filling a vacuum and the scent of rotten teeth.

In the centre of the room was a small wooden box, a little bigger than a ring box, covered in strange runes or symbols. I crept forward, my rage replaced with that same, hollow pit in my stomach. Inside the box was a tiny figurine wearing reindeer pyjamas.

21

Amy Finlay

The Diary of Elisha Kent Kane – Arctic Explorer

Christmas Eve 1852, why I should find myself at a séance in Rochester New York of all places is beyond me. Dragged here by my friend, the 'illustrious' Bernard Shank, my best friend from my college days in Virginia, the poor soul seeks to 'connect' with his fiancé who died of the influenza not six months ago. Poor Louisa. Not but twenty-one years old and to be married in the spring. Poor Bernard has taken it quite hard as one can imagine. I myself have had no such time for pursuits of the romantic kind – one is more akin to find a polar bear in the arctic than a fine lady! But after so many wild months spent in the cold confinement of the frontiers with men of rough company it would be nice to have a woman to keep my chamber warm… I must correct myself, such a thought is not becoming of a man of the word of God.

Alas, I digress ... so it was that Bernard practically begged that I accompanied him to a séance hosted by one the infamous Fox Sisters. More like Sisters of Satan! These she-devils pray on the vulnerabilities of grieving people like my poor Bernard. Naturally I was both apprehensive and sceptical of the tricks of these so-called 'psychics'. Does not the Holy word of Scripture state: 'Regard not them that have familiar spirits, neither seek after wizards, to be defiled by them; I am the LORD your God.' The upper echelons of good New York society are certainly being defiled by these unholy women. They have taken their wanton parlour games to practically every establishment in the city – even the honourable ones. Bernard claims he was invited to a select private gathering in the home of Dr Frank Astor of Rochester. It appears men of science are apparently not above the allure of such charlatans. I weep for my profession.

Thus, on a snow fallen Christmas Eve Bernard and I made the long carriage journey to Rochester. The wind was howling and snow battering our window-a scene that I could almost appreciate as beautiful had I been safely tucked up in my parlour reading a book – which, after nine long months in the arctic, is where I most desired to be.

In the carriage Bernard was restless from the apparent 'excitement' of the occasion. We were, I was told, privileged to receive such an invitation as the Fox sisters were very selective with who they took meetings with. The appeal of 'celebrities' held more interest for him than I. In the carriage Bernard was restless and kept readjusting his cravat. Finally, he sought my opinion:

'Say Friend, do you think this a fitting cravat for such an occasion?'

'Truthfully old chap I do not know what the appropriate attire *is* for such an occasion. Won't we be sitting in the dark anyway so therefore no one will *see* your cravat – let alone be in a position to pass judgement on it. The sisters certainly won't want their dirty tricks made visible to the table,' I scoffed. Bernard appeared unamused, paused, then replied:

'As I recall when you decided to travel to the Arctic, in search of the final frontiers of the earth, did not people think you mad?'

'Yes, they certainly did but I do not see how the two are related.'

'People thought you mad, people think these women are mad. Yet you are both united in a quest for discovery. You, my friend have discovered new territories unknown to any map or man. These women have also found a new way of discovering truth, a new form of communication if you will.'

'Truth!' I snarled. 'If you can term what they do to be true then I fear for your own sanity old pal.'

Bernard took it all in good humour. 'That may be your opinion, but progress is certainly being made. They have, after all, been endorsed by the great novelist Sir Robert Louis Stevenson. And I dare say if they are good enough for detective Holmes, surely they are good enough for me.'

I smirked. How could two friends be so similar but also so different? But despite the hardship he had faced Bernard was a good soul-Louisa's death had been hard on him. I just didn't know what magic he expected these women to perform. That Louisa was on the other side, not suffering, granting him permission to move on. All things I, and any reasonable person, could have comforted him with. I hoped they hadn't added some new magic tricks to their repertoire-I had visions of them trying to raise her from the dead like Lazarus with her handkerchief. Perish the thought!

I was glad to get in from the cold New York winter and into the charming festive home of Dr Astor. There was a small party of eight guests including Bernard and myself. Dr Astor, a most jovial man in his twilight years wearing a monocle, a Mrs Blanchard, also of mature age, dripping in foxes and diamonds, an unremarkable but perfectly pleasant couple in their middle age, Mr and Mrs Small. Two bachelors and business partners, a Mr and Mr Crookshank. All people seemingly of sound mind and evidently with nowhere else to be on Christmas Eve. We were served hot spiced punch in an impressive drawing room. A queer festive gathering indeed! The atmosphere was feverish; it soon became clear that I was the only one not under the spell of the Fox sisters.

'Will not Miss Maggie Fox be joining us for a drink or are we to believe that she prefers to enjoy her spirits with spirits?' I smirked.

There was a pause, followed by an anxious laugh from Bernard which eventually the rest of the party joined in with.

'No my good fellow,' stated Dr Astor, 'Miss Fox prefers not to meet our party until we assemble at table so as to get a better read on our energies.'

This was accepted as commonplace amongst our party and while I could not comprehend the energies of others, I knew mine was becoming increasingly agitated.

Alas, the clock struck eight and we sat awkwardly at the dining table. Bernard appeared so nervous and was sweating so much that at several times I had to hand him my handkerchief so he could wipe his brow.

At last, the infamous Miss Fox entered the room. I heard Mrs Small emit a small gasp. Oh, to be in the company of such a celebrity! Miss Fox, or Maggie, as she introduced herself was evidently a very beautiful woman. That was the conclusion any reasonable man could deduce. This no doubt aided her in her craft. To say she was captivating was true, when she spoke all eyes were on her. Petite, long black hair, pale complexion, dark eyes.

She sat down at the table and introduced herself as Maggie Fox. We were gathered together in the pursuit of communicating with whatever spirits were open to communicating with us tonight. There were two rules, keep the circle closed by holding hands and if a spirit joins no one should talk to them except her. She couldn't say how long the circle would last but it depended on who showed themselves to us.

I snarled again, perhaps too loudly, and found myself on the receiving end of a kick in the shin from Bernard.

We all held hands. Miss Fox asked, 'Is there a spirit here tonight who wishes to speak to us?'

The planchette on the board moved to 'yes'.

Naturally I was expecting Miss Fox to make the most out of her booking fee, so to have a party with no spirits willing to talk would surely be bad for business – and a short evening indeed.

'Good heavens,' cried one of the Crookshank bachelors.

'What is your name, spirit?' Miss Fox continued.

The planchette spelt out M-A-J-O-R.

'Major, thank you for joining us. Do you have a message for someone here?'

The planchette moved to 'yes'.

'Can you spell who it is you want to communicate with?'

The planchette moved and spelt out M-I-N-O-R.

A chill ran up my spine while the rest of the party looked puzzled.

'Minor?' Asked Miss Fox. Again, the planchette moved to 'yes.'

'Minor? Does the name Minor mean anything to anyone?'

My heart sank in my chest. Everyone looked around puzzled, suddenly I saw the slow dawn of realisation reach Bernard's face. Wide eyed he looked at me, incredulous as the board moved.

Suddenly one of the candles in the room was hastily extinguished by a large gust of wind that seemingly came from nowhere.

'Major wants to communicate directly through me,' Miss Fox said quickly. She looked directly at me, her intuition leading her to 'Minor.'

The colour in my face drained. For I myself was the 'minor' being referenced...

There were looks of surprise from the party. I blushed under the weight of the communal stare. 'I can feel the cold, the snow, I can barely see anything. A blizzard. He's outside in some snowy conditions.'

All of a sudden, I am there again. That terrible day – or was it night? Days and nights were the same in that God forsaken place. The snow so thick that sight evades you. The wind howls so loudly you think you will never experience silence ever again. Keep your eyes ahead on Major at all times…

Miss Fox's face was contorted, and she was shivering as though she was cold. The room seemed to have dropped in temperature quite significantly. A chill ran up my back. Every hair on my body seemed to stand on edge. I couldn't breathe. There were a million men called John-but how could she know of my nickname, the names shared by John and I alone, Ursa Major and Minor, the two bears in the arctic…

'Major says you have his wedding ring and it needs to go to his wife Mildred, and that you are not to feel guilty because what happened was an accident. He is at peace now.'

A cold so cold you lose all sensation – icicles on my beard, my nose. Yet John was braver than I, a pioneer, in charge and in front until, until, I lost concentration, my footing, slipped and he reached out to grab me and then he fell backwards, down that mountain, that dark devourer of souls and he was gone, claimed by the snowy abyss to lie down with the other poor souls who dance with the devil… One wrong step and it would have been me to meet my maker. No. I must not think of such awful things! To explore is to risk death, we both knew that…but John, Major – it should have been me. I was the one who fancied myself the great explorer, the best of all men, willing to face death in the pursuit of knowledge. But as I saw Major's blurry body fade into the dark snow I felt nothing but relief that it was him and not I going into that dark place where there is no rest…

She spoke the words so plainly and with such confidence I could barely look at her, though she held my gaze with such a quiet confidence as I have yet to encounter in a woman. I had in my pocket John's wedding ring which, I am ashamed to say, I have avoided returning to his widow for fear that my selfishness will somehow be evidence on my face. My youthful cockiness cost a great man his soul, left a wife a widow and a child without a father.

I was suffocating in that room. With those words I am ashamed to say I hastily stood up and quickly exited the room without a single regard that I had broken the circle.

The whole way home I could barely speak let alone look at Bernard. That I was an explorer was fairly well known, that many people lose their lives in the arctic is to be deduced, but how, how did she know about the rest, the full shameful sordid tale?

There was little point in going to bed that Christmas Eve for I was tormented by Major's body falling into that great abyss. Every time I closed my eyes, I felt I was joining him, falling deeper and deeper into the blackness…

The next day on Christmas morning I somehow steadied myself and made my way to Major's house. I was as white as the morning snow. I returned the wedding ring to Mildred who was delighted to have some small part of her husband back. Two things were now clear in my mind.

That communication with the dead was possible.

And I had to see Miss Fox again.

Author Bios

Hadyn Adams is a retired educationalist who has self-published three novels and who has had various poems published in magazines and on-line publications. He lives in Colchester in the United Kingdom.

Tim Newton Anderson
http://atjentertainments.wordpress.com

Alice Baburek is an avid reader, determined writer and animal lover. She lives with her wife and four canine companions. Retired, she challenges herself to become an unforgettable emerging voice.

Evan Baughfman is a Southern California playwright/author. His plays are published through Heuer Publishing, YouthPLAYS, Next Stage Press, and Drama Notebook. Evan has also found success writing prose, his work found recently in anthologies by Graveside Press and No Bad Books Press. Evan's own books include: *The Emaciated Man*, *Vanishing of the 7th Grade*, *Bad for Your Teeth*, and *Try Not to Die in a Dark Fairy Tale*. More info available at amazon.com/author/evanbaughfman

Ria Cabral https://www.riacabralauthor.com/

Amy Finlay holds a PhD in Irish literature from Queen's university Belfast. Interested in the liminal space between fantasy and gothic, Finlay is an avid reader of horror and women's fiction.

Sarah Hozumi is a writer who has lived near Tokyo for about 16 years. To read short stories she's had published, and to read her blog mostly about all things Japan, please visit sarahhozumi.com. You can also follow her on Facebook at sarahjhozumi and Instagram at @author.sarah.hozumi.

Kevin MacAlan lives in Co Waterford. He has an MA in Creative Writing, and has contributed to many journals, including, An Áitiúil, Howl, Stripes, Bindweed, Datura, The Madrid Review, The Martello, and The Wild Umbrella. He was longlisted for The National Poetry Competition 2023 and The Fish Poetry Prize 2024
    Instagram: instagram.com/kevinmacalan
    BlueSky: kevinmacalan.bsky.social
    Twitter: x.com/kevininireland

Callum J. McCready is an Irish artist. Previously based out of Fisterra and Galicia, he has recently returned to Belfast. When not working by day he moonlights as a writer.
    Over fifty poems of his work have been published in numerous journals including *A New Ulster*, *Bindweed Magazine* and *The Galway Review*. He has a number of projects in the works and an intention to cross over into other disciplines.
    When not bound by the ball-and-chain of his desk he enjoys gardening, exercising, reading, listening to music, watching movies and spending time with family and friends.

Nathan McKee is a writer from Belfast, specialising in Audio Dramas. He has written for the Sci-Fi Mystery podcast Oakbridge, and is writer/creator of the upcoming 32 Old Mill Lane: A Christmas Ghost Story. Nathan enjoys writing mysteries with supernatural elements.
    nmckeesound.bsky.social
    https://www.instagram.com/32oldmilllane/

Eolas Pellor's work has appeared in a variety of online and print publications. He is an autistic former reporter, who taught a wide variety of subjects in inner-city schools for nearly 30 years before retiring.

https://sites.google.com/view/eolaspellorwriter/home#h.tarw5zu9jdl5

Subham Rai is an emerging writer from Kolkata, India. His work has appeared in Strange Horizons, Macrame Literary Journal, Cohesion Press (SNAFU: Contagion), and Zoetic Press (Mosscap's Ledger), with additional stories in Graveside Press (Kosmos Obscura). Forthcoming works include Bread Over the Line in Consequence Forum, The Salem Shadow in Graveside Press's Witchcraft Anthology, and Margaret Hollow in Vellum Mortis. Find him at:
https://linktr.ee/subhamraiauthor.

Matthew J. Richardson lives in Scotland and has a Professional Doctorate in Education. He has stories in Gold Dust magazine, Literally Stories, Close to the Bone, McStorytellers, Fiction Junkies, Soft Cartel, Whatever Keeps the Lights On, Flashback Fiction, CafeLit, Best Microfiction 2021, Writer's Egg, Idle Ink, Down in the Dirt, and Shooter. Matthew blogs at www.matthewjrichardson.com.

Leilanie Stewart is an award-winning author and poet from Belfast, Northern Ireland. She writes ghost and psychological horror as well as experimental verse. In addition to promoting her own work and editing *Bindweed Anthologies*, Leilanie teaches creative writing to sixth form students and works in a library, where she indulges her passion for books.
https://leilaniestewart.com/

Monti Sturzaker can be found wherever there are words or walking her rescue dogs, Echo and Whisper. She's previously published in The Fantastic Other, Memezine, and Indie Bites.

Amber Willis is a student of paleontology and biology. She is a collector of crap (literally! Coprolites, aka, fossilized poop) that adorns her bookshelves. She lives with her frogs and a turtle on a mountainside in the middle of nowhere in North Carolina. She is a welder by day and stalks bats and frogs in their habitats at night.

Find Amber on Facebook:
www.facebook.com/profile.php?id=61580281555216

About Bindweed Anthologies

Bindweed Magazine was first launched in April 2016 as a quarterly paperback issue publishing poetry and fiction from new and established authors worldwide. Issues 1-8 were published between 2016 and 2018. The publication then reverted to *Bindweed Online* as an annual ezine, publishing poetry and fiction on the magazine homepage for Issues 9 to 12 from 2019 to 2022.

In June 2022, *Bindweed Anthologies* was launched, with the biannual *Midsummer Madness* and *Winter Wonderland* editions, publishing in both Kindle eBook and paperback formats during 2022 to 2024.

Bindweed launched a new format for the 2025 anthologies, publishing *Withywind* in May 2025, followed by the seasonally themed *White Witch's Hat & other Yuletide ghost stories* in November 2025.

Check our submission guidelines for more exciting anthologies coming in 2026.

Submission guidelines are at:
https://bindweedmagazine.wordpress.com/submission-guidelines

Back issues of Bindweed Anthologies can be found at the National Library of Ireland

We're proudly listed on Duotrope:
https://duotrope.com/magazine/bindweed-magazine-anthology-24250

Printed in Dunstable, United Kingdom